THE END *of the* BEGINNING

Sybil Nocroft Book One

Carl Douglass

Neurosurgeon who writes with gripping realism

PO Box 221974 Anchorage, Alaska 99522-1974
books@publicationconsultants.com
www.publicationconsultants.com

ISBN 978-1-59433-452-8
eBook ISBN 978-1-59433-453-5
Library of Congress Catalog Card Number: 2014934073

Manufactured in the United States of America.

Dedication

To my family

Disclaimer

The Sybil Series is a work of fiction and should not be construed as representing real persons, places, or events. Some names of real persons and places appear but only for the purpose of creating a setting in the real world or as a mention of historical circumstances. None of the real people or the real places were actually involved in the fictional writing. All of the events described were created from the author's imagination.

Books by Carl Douglass

FICTION

Last Phoenix A Novel of Betrayal and Revenge, A Story of the CIA's Phoenix Program

Saga of a Neurosurgeon Series
Young Coyote: Garven Wilsonhulme's Way to Success-No Quarter Asked and None Given

Anything Goes: Garven Wilsonhulme Takes on All Comers in the Jungle of Modern Competition

Heaven and Hell: Garven Wilsonhulme Takes on All Comers in the Jungle of Modern Competition

Long Climb: Young M.D., Garven Wilsonhulme, Fngaged in a Social Poker Game of Winner Takes All

Academia: The Law of the Jungle: Surgeon in Training, Garven Wilsonhulme, Fang-and-Claw Competition for Glory

The Vulture and the Phoenix: Neurosurgeon, Garven Wilsonhulme, the Final Great Fight

All in Jest: Renowned Neurosurgeon in the Fight of Her Life

Gog and Magog: Yawm al-Qiyamah, Yawm al-Din, The Day of Judgment

Finders Keepers, Losers Weep: A Novel of Innocence Betrayed and the Search for Restitution

Sheep Dog and The Wolf: A Story of Terrorism and Response, and the Sheep Dogs Who Protect

Trojan Horse in the Belly of the Beast, Three Books
Though They Come From the Ends of the Earth
Dancing with the Devil
Trojan Horse in the Belly of the Beast

NOVELLAS

The End of the Beginning	*Secrets and Scandals*
Uncharted Country, Uncertain Future	*Decisions*
Secrets	*Running with the Big Dogs*

NONFICTION

On Evolution The Origin of Selection, Order, Progression, and Diversity—out of print
   Something About Religion—out of print

Chapter One

S ybil Norcroft, M.D., Ph.D., F.A.C.S. was stung by her first defeat in her career at Joseph Noble Memorial Hospital. With the new federal Accountable Care Act provisions taking hold and the experience of surgeons at scores of other hospitals winning the right to be paid for taking emergency room call, Sybil had presumed that her negotiations with the hospital administration would be an easy win; and she would regain her popularity with the other surgeons on the staff. Instead; it was a fiasco. Not only did the administration refuse to pay surgeons a salary for ER work, but they were adamant about continuing the time-honored policy that to have hospital privileges, a surgeon had to take regular call.

When she threatened to leave her practice at the hospital and take her partners and their patients with them, Michael Strong, the hospital administrator, replied tersely, "Go ahead."

Sybil, a statuesque tall movie-star level beauty, with long, lustrous blond hair, but one with brains, knew she was beat. The hospital's decision meant having to agree to be up nights seeing people who were not sick as well as people who were;

but none of whom had insurance; and none of them ever paid the surgeon's bill. That was minor in comparison to the heavy risk of ending up with a malpractice suit by a patient with nothing to lose and the potential to win what amounted to the malpractice lottery.

Her week was about to get worse. Dr. Norcroft's office manager knocked softly on Sybil's private office door. That quiet knock meant that a member of her office staff was cringing outside the door afraid of the explosion that was certain to erupt when the boss saw the return address on the envelope.

"Come in," Sybil said flatly dreading what harbinger of evil her employee was carrying.

"Sorry," Gladys said. "I didn't dare wait too long. You always say you want bad news right away."

"Whatever possessed me to say such a dumb thing?" Sybil said with a wan smile.

Gladys handed the doctor the envelope. It was slightly damp from her sweaty hand.

It took only a glance on Sybil's part. The return address told her that the expensive envelope came from Stewart, Bel Geddes, and Loughlin, Attorneys at Law—the law firm from hell. Gladys slid back out of the room watching Dr. Norcroft's usually placid face turn scarlet and to crinkle up into a ferocious mask of wrath.

"Sorry," Gladys said again and made a hasty exit.

The letterhead was inaccurate. Both Stewart and Loughlin were dead. Their names on the firm's letterhead and door gave some needed credibility to the firm now headed by the man known in the legal profession as the most successful and richest malpractice attorney in history and by the medical profession as Barratry Paul. It hardly mattered who the plaintiff was or what the issue was; Sybil knew that she was

in for another terrible, insulting, demeaning, and bruising
battle with her nemesis. This was her eighth time to be sued
by Paul. He never learned from defeat; she had prevailed
six times, and once she had been forced by the malpractice
insurance company to settle in a case which she, her lawyers,
and even the insurance company executives, admitted was a
slam-dunk for the defense. It was just too expensive for the
company to defend and was cheaper to settle no matter what
damage was done to the doctor's reputation.

She pushed the button to summon Gladys.

"Yes, Ma'am," Gladys said timidly.

"Oh, don't be such a sissy," Sybil said with a small smile
meant to dispel the sulfurous vapors in her office. "Just send
the stupid letter on to my lawyer, Susan McIntosh, at Schmidt
and Tarkington. They're used to getting letters directed at me
from the man whose name I can't even bear to say. Too bad
somebody doesn't just bump him off. Maybe I'll have to take
matters into my own hands."

Gladys checked out her boss's face as she took the letter.
She knew that Dr. Norcroft was kidding, but her face did
show it. She knew how much Dr. Norcroft hated Paul Bel
Geddes, and guessed that the Snow Queen's vehement outburst had to be entirely a joke. It had to be.

Sybil did not have to read the letter to know what was
going on. The patient named as the plaintiff, was Jeffery
Mortenson. He had been brought into the emergency room
on one of Sybil's nights on call (of course). She had been
extremely tired and was out of sorts from having to deal with
patients who must have crawled out from under a rock to
come to the ER with their back pain complaints.

Poor Jeffery. The young man—a newly-wed—arrived
by ambulance accompanied by his small attractive wife,

Annette. Both of them were twenty-five years old and were dressed in work clothes, but a quick glance by Sybil told her that they were Yuppies who had gotten into serious trouble. Jeffery was not accustomed to manual labor, especially not to construction. He and Annette had purchased a fixer-upper in a rural area which had been moved to the location by the previous owners from a city location. The house was still up on jacks and six-by-six supports which held it about nine inches off the ground. Annette had discovered that their new little dream home was being eaten away by skunks, badgers, and raccoons which were burrowing into the floor from underneath.

Jeffery—the frugal and newly industrious young husband—collected varmint traps and a rake and proceeded to wriggle his way under the house. It was tight and uncomfortable, and the stench of the animal urine and droppings was overwhelming. He was filthy and recoiled from the dreadful conditions under his house. He backed out in a hurry and heedlessly knocked one of the support blocks out from the edge of the house with his foot. The house sagged and made it a very tight squeeze for Jeffery to get out. He wriggled and writhed and managed to get his entire body except for his head out from under the heavy house. His last move was to swing the rake around to move it out with him. Unfortunately, the rake took out another block, and the house fell on the newlywed's head crushing his skull. Amazingly, there was just enough support from the uneven ground that he was not killed immediately, and was conscious when a construction crew accompanying the EMTs jacked up the house and freed him.

In the ER, Sybil examined Jeffery and found his scalp riddled with lacerations and the man's skull was broken into a mosaic of odd sized and shaped pieces of bones on both sides of the calvarium. He was alert enough to give a rambling history and was able to move all four extremities. He had lost a copious amount of blood and was beginning to fade away.

"He needs to have an MRI," Sybil told Annette, who was distraught and almost hysterical from looking at the devastation that had once been her handsome husband's head.

Sybil continued, "And we will have to operate to put him back together again as soon as possible."

"Do whatever you have to, Dr. Norcroft. Please save him. I think you know that I am a malpractice attorney, but please save him. I promise I won't sue you. Just take good care him. He's all I have."

Knowing that she would have to operate and that the MRI was needed only to determine the extent of brain injury and internal bleeding, Sybil delivered the world's most thorough informed consent presentation.

"Any questions?" she asked.

"Will he be all right?"

"It's too soon to know, Mrs. Mortensen. He'll survive the operation, but I can't say how much brain damage he has suffered or how much function he will retain. His wounds are filled with embedded farm dirt and animal feces. It is likely, even probable, that we will have to treat an infection. This is going to be a long process."

"Just do your best. That's all I ask. I know you are the best. You don't have to worry about being sued."

"*Of course I don't*," Sybil groaned to herself, guessing that the odds were ten to one against her.

"And we don't have any insurance, but we'll pay you, no matter how much it costs. Just give Jeffery the very best care and don't spare any expense."

It was all Sybil could do to keep from laughing.

"And pigs will fly over to my office to deliver the payment," Sybil muttered sarcastically to herself as she left for the locker room to change into scrubs.

The operation was an all-night ordeal. Sybil had to wash large amounts of dirt, pebbles, and animal raisins out of the torn scalp and off the broken pieces of skull. A few tears had occurred in the dura, and there were bits of dirt on and in the brain. Sybil ended up having to put in a dural graft and to take out every bone fragment and to wash it individually with antibiotic solution and to replace it as a mosaic of separate pieces to allow room for the inevitable swelling. She had to undermine the scalp on the entire head to try to get a watertight closure, but it was futile. She ended up having to put a deep graft of dural substitute over the bare areas and to create a large full thickness vascularized graft of hair bearing skin to cover an area where Jeffery's own scalp could not reach. Dr. Norcroft finally had to resort to placing a patch of pig skin brought in from the burn unit OR to complete the coverage.

Postoperatively, the brain swelling was severe; so, Sybil had Jeffery put into an induced coma for three weeks. The infection she feared occurred; it turned out to be raccoon e-coli in origin. Jeffery was young and healthy and after three months weathered the worst of it. He spent the next eight months in rehab. Finally, two years and three scalp restructuring operations later, he was released from Dr. Norcroft's care except for yearly clinic visits. He had lost ten or fifteen points from his I.Q. and was a little slow in getting speech out but was otherwise remarkably well given all that he had been through.

The day after he was discharged from rehab, Sybil received the intent to sue for malpractice letter from the law firm of Annette Crenshaw and Paul Bel Geddes. Since the letters came in a Stewart, Bel Geddes, and Loughlin, Attorneys at

Law envelope, it was obvious that Paul Bel Geddes would be sitting first chair. To her confidants on the surgical staff, and her two partners in her Joseph Noble Neurosurgery Associates group, David Pennyman and Adele Sanchez-Hernandez, she vented her rage with intemperate invectives and some outlandishly extreme vows of revenge that made her feel better and which no one took seriously.

Sybil and her husband, Charles Daniels—billionaire agribusiness CEO—attended a charity function New Year's Eve black-tie party in the ballroom of the Chateau de Eugenie Hotel in Los Angeles. Between the entrée and dessert, a charity auction was held. The chief of police, the archbishop of the diocese, and the Danielses had a good-natured contest as to who would end up making the highest bids for several fairly mundane offerings. Sybil made a fairly extravagant bid that everyone felt was as far as the bids could climb.

The auctioneer banged his gavel, "going once, going twice…" and was interrupted by a man and his much younger blond and pneumatic wife who were very well known in charity circles.

Ann-Margaret Bel Geddes announced that, "we'll up the bid by $10,000."

It seemed late, a bit out of place, and more than a bit crass, especially from a girl showing much too much of her plastic surgeon's work.

The guests at Sybil's table emitted a chorus of none-too-subtle groans, and Ann-Margaret's husband jumped up to her rescue. He beamed his patented chicklet glow-in-the-dark smile at Sybil and her husband.

"So the billionaires over at table three don't like to be trumped by us lowly middle-class citizens. Too bad, we'll just up the ante another $20,000. We won't be suffering any too

15

much financial loss. I will collect all of that and more when I finish defending the latest poor victim of the ruthless Snow Queen over there."

The partygoers who did not know about the Sybil and Paul war of attrition gasped at the gross discourtesy which was likely to ruin the gala evening. Those who did know Paul considered it nothing short of what they might have expected but nonetheless crass.

Charles put his hand on Sybil's forearm and put his index finger to his lips. She angrily jerked her hand away and snarled, "Don't patronize me, Charles. That bottom feeder has gone too far. Somebody needs to do something about him."

The guests at the table raised their eyebrows at her quiet but venomous outburst. The chief of police looked askance at her, and the archbishop shook his head. It was perhaps fair for her to be angry, but her verbal implied threat was unchristian nonetheless.

"Sorry, Charles," Sybil said, "but I can't stand to be in the same room with that dirt-bag and his floozy. Please take me home."

The Danielses made a fairly obvious exit, and the sophisticated crowd took notice.

Chapter Two

At one o'clock in the morning a week later, homicide Detective Lieutenant Anson Burger took the call from the 911 operator.

"This is Marie from the emergency call center. Neighbors reported a shot fired at a Bel Aire residence. Unis were called and found a dead man, obviously a murder. My supervisor told me that you had the call."

"Lucky me," Burger said. "Is it going to get worse? Is it a celebrity, perish the very thought?"

"Sort of, Detective. Apparently the victim is a multi-millionaire philanthropist lawyer and part of the cream-of-society up there."

"Got a name?"

"Hang on a sec…Yeah, it's Paul Devon Bel Geddes. His wife is totally out of control hysterical. Be warned."

"Thanks, Marie. Hope your night goes better than mine is likely to be."

The media crews were already out in force, and it was an all-out circus by the time Burger pulled into the police parking area. He ducked under the yellow tape and walked over to the headquarters tent that had been set up on the side lawn of the palatial grounds.

Deputy Chief of Detectives Ryan Drexel looked grumpily at Burger, "Traffic, I presume?"

"Something like that, Chief. I was lights and sirens all the way as soon as I heard. What's the skinny?"

Chief Drexel filled him in with classical homicide detective brevity: "Shotgun to the back of the head. Not much left front or back. Wife identified him from a couple of tattoos and a set of very expensive teeth. Looks like forced entry through a back bathroom window and a robbery gone bad. A secret safe had been opened, maybe under duress; and the wife says that something on the order of two mil in cash, watches, and diamonds is missing. CSIs are all over the place. The ME is holding the body until you can get a look at it and the scene. He is pretty sure that the TOD was between ten-thirty and eleven. It's all yours now. I have a mad wife at home, and I gotta get back and make my in-laws happy; so, Daphne will give me some peace."

"Okay, Chief, I have it."

The scene was mostly as Chief Drexel had described it. However, there were a few details that were a bit off. One was that there were two sets of footprints in the garden dirt outside the window. The second was that the window was fairly high and would have required either a ladder or a fairly nimble athlete to succeed in getting in. There were no marks of a ladder. The wife stated that she had been out to a fashion show and a girls' night out with friends. When she returned home, she discovered the body and then promptly fell to pieces. Burger had to wait eighteen hours before he could interview the wife, and she still looked a mess and was sedated from what must have been a Valium milk shake from the looks of her. The interview yielded some useful information, despite the semi-stuporous condition of Ann-Margaret Bel Geddes.

Mrs. Bel Geddes was very forthcoming and waived her rights to an attorney. She told Burger up-front that she was the sole beneficiary of her husband's will because his four children from previous marriages (five of them) were all estranged from their father. She was quite precise about her alibi, and Burger found a timeline that would have allowed her to have slipped out, done the dastardly deed, faked the robbery, and gotten back to the girls' party without attracting much attention. She willingly permitted the detectives and CSIs to take her shoes to compare them to the imprint outside the bathroom window. Burger's initial impression was that she was not smart enough to plan and execute a clever murder and fake robbery, but you never knew.

The Bel Geddes's did not own a gun. Burger and a squad of junior rank detectives canvassed the neighborhood and interviewed Bel Geddes's two new partners and found out that both of them were angry at Paul for refusing to grant them full financial partnership or to have their names included with his as legal attorneys with the prestigious standing that afforded. He had refused to pay for a key-man insurance policy; so, they had nothing to gain by his death. Burger learned another very interesting fact about the deceased. He had taken on only the highest potential paying clients during the last four years, but he continued to keep control of a schlocky branch of the firm in East L.A. which served workman's comp, minor criminal matters—mostly drug involved—family law, and slip-and-fall cases. The lawyers were down and outers, had drug problems themselves, and some had question marks about their legal licenses. They uniformly hated their boss who treated them like *untermenschen*. A few of them had made threats in public towards Bel Geddes when they were in their cups.

Burger and his five full-time detectives spent many hours every day interviewing lists of disgruntled defendants Bel Geddes had sued over the years and more than a few of his own clients whom he might have shorted on the compensation that came out of their successful trials. Ann-Margaret told him about the doctor—Sybil Norcroft—and her threats.

"She did it, you know. She did it. She thinks she is so hot that she don't have to obey the law. She hated my Paul for no reason. She is a bad doctor, and Paul proved it. She got mad and made threats. Ask anybody. She did it. You'll see."

Burger did his leg work very thoroughly. After a month, he got around to Sybil.

To put her out of her comfort zone, Detective Burger had Sybil come to the LAPD Robbery and Homicide Division offices still operated from an annex of the Old Parker Center for her interview. She came with two criminal attorneys.

The detective, the two lawyers, and Sybil entered in the small, uninviting, utilitarian metal walled interview room.

"Have a seat," Burger said.

"Thank you so much," Sybil said making little effort to curtail her sarcasm.

The older of the two attorneys introduced himself and his co-counsel, "Jack Henley, and Rupert Ortega, criminal defense attorneys from the firm of Schmidt, Principle, Tarkington, and Henley."

Sybil, her attorneys, and the detective exchanged business cards.

"Now, what is this all about?" Henley asked, setting a business-like tone.

"I have some questions for Ms. Norcroft in the matter of the death of Paul bel Geddes, Esq."

"As a matter of clarification, it's Doctor Norcroft, Detective."

"Umm hum," Burger mouthed, "my first question is quite straightforward. Would you please give me a rundown on your background?"

Sybil handed Burger a copy of her curriculum vitae and a copy of the glossy professional brochure the office handed out to new patients.

"I am currently the chief of surgery at Joseph Noble Memorial Hospital and have an active neurosurgery practice. In addition I am on several professional and philanthropic boards and am the current president of the American Professional Women's Association and president-elect of the Los Angeles County Republican Party."

"Do you know Paul Bel Geddes?"

"I did. I have learned that he is now dead."

"Thank you," Burger said with a tight-lipped expression that hinted at a level of sarcasm comparable to that of Sybil's first comment.

"How would you characterize your relationship with the late Mr. bel Geddes?"

"Professional and correct."

"Did you threaten him?"

"Don't answer that," Henley said.

Burger nodded, and his disdain for both the doctor and her lawyer showed.

"Was your relationship cordial?"

Henley whispered to Sybil.

"It was professional and correct. He was a lawyer, and I am a doctor. He represented plaintiffs who filed suit against me.

"One suit?"

"Several?"

"Who won those suits?"

"With one exception, I won them all. That exception was a case that my malpractice insurance company insisted on settling despite my strong objections. The executives of the company admitted that I was in the right, but they would not pursue the case because of the cost they would incur."

"Did you and do you harbor a grudge against Mr. Bel Geddes?"

"No."

"No?"

"No."

Burger shook his head to indicate his complete disbelief.

"Did you once kidnap him, drug him, and get him to his office in a state of profound lack of self-control to sabotage his performance as the attorney opposing you?"

"No," she said without a glimmer of change in her calm facial expression.

She was good, Burger had to admit.

"Where on earth did you come up with that outlandish idea, Detective?" Henley asked heatedly.

"I'll ask the questions," Burger said.

Henley rolled his eyes.

"Ms. Norcroft, is that your entire answer?"

Henley moved to interrupt, but Sybil put her hand on his forearm to prevent Henley from protesting again about her being disrespected.

"It's all right Jack. I'm used to being treated shabbily by people of his ilk."

If it bothered Burger, he did not show it. He was a large, powerfully muscled man with a tough but maybe ruggedly handsome face topped with a full head of curly black hair. He did not get intimidated, especially not by fragile beautiful starlet types.

"Did you attend a New Year's Eve charity function at the Chateau de Eugenie Hotel in Los Angeles this year, Ms. Norcroft?"

He looked to see if the doctor would wince. She didn't.

"Yes."

"Did you have a face-to-face confrontation with Mr. Bel Geddes at that gathering?"

"He approached me and was disrespectful at that time, yes."

"And did you threaten him?"

"No."

"I have a number of unimpeachable witnesses who reported for the record that you said, "That bottom feeder has gone too far. Somebody needs to do something about him." And did you not refer to him as a "bottom feeder"?"

Burger was reading from his murder book—the standard handwritten case-documentation notes kept by all detectives in the Robbery-Homicide Division.

"Something like that."

"Sounds like a threat to me."

"You're wrong."

"How am I wrong?"

"The direct intent of my comment, my outburst, if you will, was that some sane person needed to get the man under control. He had recently launched yet another frivolous law suit against me and was using the occasion to tarnish my reputation. He was being thoroughly reprehensible and unprofessional. There was certainly no intention on my part to make a genuine serious threat against his person."

Burger could envision the ice-water circulating through the woman's veins. She answered him with an entirely dispassionate tone of voice and facial expression.

"Do you dispute the reports of your "outburst" as you put it? You were witnessed to do so by the archbishop of Los Angeles and the Assistant Chief of the LAPD RHD, among others."

"I believe both of those men to be credible; but I did not intend any serious threat; and I am sure they did not consider my angry comments as anything more than a retort coming from an exasperated person."

"Umm hum," mused Burger almost theatrically.

"Do you have an office manager named Gladys Stevenson, Ms. Norcroft?"

"Yes."

"Would it surprise you to learn that she reluctantly informed me that you said…he checked his murder book notes… 'They're used to getting letters directed at me from the man whose name I can't even bear to say. Too bad somebody doesn't just bump him off. Maybe I'll have to take matters into my own hands.'"

"*Mea culpa*," Sybil said. "I was mad. Mr. Bel Geddes has had a vendetta out for me for more than a decade, and I had a moment of weakness and spoke from my gut and not my brain. It was silly; and again, nobody took that outburst as a serious threat. Besides I was referring to getting protection—legal protection—from my malpractice attorney, a Ms. Susan McIntosh."

"Perhaps," said Burger looking at her with steely detective eyes.

"Was the suit against you terminated as a result of the murder of Mr. Bel Geddes, Doctor?"

"Not to my knowledge."

Burger snorted, "Then let me be the first to inform you. The other attorneys in his law firm informed me that they have no intention of pursuing this latest suit."

"Firmer minds have prevailed, apparently," said Sybil and continued to meet Burger's eyes with a direct deadpan gaze devoid of blinking.

"Um hummh," countered Burger.

There was a short pause when no one spoke.

"Are we done here?" Jack Henley asked.

"Just about. I have a couple of more questions. Did you murder Paul Devon Bel Geddes, Ms. Norcroft?"

"Certainly not."

"Did you hire someone to kill Mr. Bel Geddes? You have plenty of money and motive. Confess and put your soul at rest."

"I am not a believer in souls, Detective. I am at peace, and I sleep just fine at night, thank you—the result of an innocent conscience."

"Where were you on the night of January 7th this year between the hours of ten and midnight."

"At home in bed with my husband, Charles Daniels."

"I questioned him, and he confirmed your alibi—big surprise."

"Do we really need the sarcasm, Detective?" protested Henley.

"Mr. Henley, mark my words, we will check out that alibi as completely as is possible. I can tell you that the department is exercising a search warrant on Ms. Norcroft's home, car, and office as we speak. If we find GSR on her clothes, we will arrest her before the day is out." He turned to Sybil and said, "This is a chance for you to come clean, maybe escape the needle. If I get word of gunshot residue on your clothes before you make a full admission, we will push for murder in the first and for the death penalty."

"Search away, Detective. I have nothing to hide. I hope you are a professional not so in need of a high profile media arrest that you will fake the evidence."

It was an insult, and Burger reacted angrily, "That is beneath contempt, a slur on me and on the LAPD. You have enemies now, little lady, watch your step."

His face was flushed, and he was gritting his teeth.

"Is that a threat, Detective? It sure sounds like a serious threat, doesn't it, Dr. Norcroft?" asked an angry Jack Henley.

"Give him some slack, Mr. Henley. I don't think he was serious. He just lost his temper and made a sort of threat that could be misconstrued if taken out of context. Isn't that a likely explanation, Detective?" Sybil said, her voice dripping with irony.

"For the record, it's lieutenant. That's all for today," Burger said, "but don't leave town. You have not seen the last of me."

"Oh, Lieutenant. I am perfectly willing to be tested for gunshot residue on my person and on my clothing right this minute," said Sybil.

"Too late," said Burger.

"That's either sloppy police work or an admission of defeat, Detective Burger. I know enough about forensic science that sometimes remnants of the residue can persist for months and through several washing cycles. I *want* you to test me. Subject me and my clothing—all of it—to particle analysis by scanning electron microscopy/energy dispersive x-ray spectrometry. That's the latest technology, I understand. I am perfectly innocent. You well know that, and you are barking up the wrong tree. We are leaving; so, you won't waste any more time in the search for the real killer."

With that, Sybil and her attorneys got up and walked out of the room without a backward glance at the angry detective.

Chapter Three

Lieutenant Burger made his fifth weekly report to Chief Drexel and the rest of the detectives in the Chief of D's morning briefing.

"We have a legion of suspects in the Bel Geddes murder. There are disgruntled employees, angry people who lost fortunes to clients of Bel Geddes, angry people who lost their cases because of what they perceive as neglect and attorney malpractice. He has five ex-wives and four grown children who hate him and his new trophy wife. Speaking of her, on the surface she would have seem to have the best motive and the best alibi; she inherits his estate and his insurance; but she has more than a dozen people—some of them reasonable citizen types—who swear that she was elsewhere when the crime occurred. The worst possibility we're facing is that this could be a simple robbery gone wrong—there's nearly two million bucks worth of cash, expensive watches, and jewelry gone from his safe. His wife swears that he must have had Alzheimer's because he was forever leaving the safe door open.

"We have a ton of work to do, and we need more cops. We will have to have maybe five or six hundred interviews before we get done with this. We have to hit every fence and pawn shop in the state and in Nevada, at least."

Chief Drexel interrupted, "Burger, we have to get ahead of this thing. The mayor is on my back, and now I'm on yours. Find us a perp; get an arrest; let's get this out of the media who are after our hides. I want them to put us out as the protectors of the city who are successfully taking killers off the streets. Got it?"

"I got it, Chief, but we are running up against a brick wall—or more aptly—against a sea of suspects. It is going to take time to sift through all of them—a lot of shoe leather and overtime."

"Overtime?"

"Yes, sir. Sorry about that, but there is a ton of work to do."

"You like to work alone, but the mayor says for you to get a partner, maybe two. He wants this solved. And, yes, I have the Commissioner's okay for overtime. Now, I have a couple of final questions. Have you got a gut feeling at least about who did this?"

"I hate gut feelings, Chief. But, I know this is getting to be long. My two main suspects are a doctor, name of Norcroft, who has had a history with the deceased and who has publicly threatened him. The other is the trophy wife who inherits everything upon her husband's death. She does not seem to be all that broken up about the man's passing. Little birdies tell me she has already found a nice boy-toy to comfort her. Besides, she has an alibi I can't break."

"What about the doctor?"

"Good on motive, and her alibi is weak—depends entirely on her billionaire husband who is willing to swear on a stack of Bibles that they were at home making the two-backed monster during the time in question."

"Bring 'em both in and put 'em on the rack. Get one of them to break. Meanwhile, we'll get together a task force to filter through your big list and then to question them. Bring 'em into Parker Center at half hour intervals. We'll make it a marathon day. I want this case closed and the mayor off my back."

"You got it, Chief. I get the thing going as soon as I get out of the briefing."

"Don't let me keep you."

As soon as Sybil and her attorneys left the interview room at Parker Center Annex, they met with the private investigator the attorneys hired the day before. He had beat the cops to the punch on her clothes. He had all of her wardrobe examined for GSR and brought back to the house before the LAPD search warrant was served. The lab he chose was regularly used by the FBI; so, its findings would be above reproach. The preliminary findings indicated no GSR—no evidence of burned, unburned, or partially burned propellant (gunpowder), no metal trace. GSR contains metal particulates including lead, copper, brass, zinc, or nickel from jacketing material. The tests for lead styphnate—the initiating explosive—barium nitrate—the oxidizer—or antimony sulfide—all common traceable ingredients of GSR—were negative, but the lab insisted that it would not put out a final report for a week or more. Sybil and Charles gave the private investigation company carte blanche to follow the investigation wherever it led and gave the lead investigator a blank check with no limits.

Charles and Sybil recognized that she was being seriously considered as a suspect in the murder, and that LAPD investigators were known for their myopic viewpoints. If there was a husband, he did it; if they found a high-profile individual with motive, means, and opportunity, he or she would be a good second-best subject of interest. Burger and his task force drew blanks from their marathon interviews, which stretched into a 48 hour exercise in endurance. That left him with Ann-Margaret Bel Geddes—the ditsy trophy suicide-blond spouse—whose alibi was unbreakable, and Dr. Sybil Norcroft-Daniels, who certainly had motive, means, and maybe opportunity. He considered her alibi to be pretty flimsy; her husband was certainly anything but objective and did not seem to Burger to be entirely forthcoming. The pressure on the detective was becoming unbearable. He was frustrated that his GSR lab studies were still pending, and the house search by the CSIs and his detective squad had produced zilch. The canvass of pawnshops and the shakedowns of confidential informants and gang bangers was also useless.

It was crunch time. Burger scheduled an appointment with Len Prentiss, the senior deputy DA, and together they made a decision. It was one neither of them felt entirely comfortable with, but it was the best they could come up with. Neither woman suspect was the least bit of a sympathetic character, and the one they chose was going to create a typical Hollywood scandal and circus.

Doug Howard was the only early-bird journo in the now dwindling reporter pool at the *Los Angeles Times*. He had survived all of the cuts thus far because he produced good solid news, had great confidential sources and a Pulitzer; and he knew where all of the skeletons were buried. As always, he checked the on-line overnight police reports first and hit pay-dirt. Detective Lieutenant Anson Burger of the Robbery-

Homicide Detective Division had filed his preliminary report on an arrest in the "Super-Lawyer Murder" as it had come to be known. The investigation was still ongoing, but the detectives had gone to the palatial home of the famous woman neurosurgeon, Sybil Norcroft, at midnight and arrested her. They took her husband, billionaire agri-business exec, Charles Daniels, in for questioning as a material witness and for possible obstruction of justice.

Doug got on the horn and on the internet and called out the troops. One unit headed for the Daniels home, and the other—which Doug led—went to the central lock-up. They were determined to get a statement from Burger and, if at all possible, from the perps. Doug's usual phenomenal good luck was in force that day, and he met Charles Daniels coming out of the front door of Central Booking with his lawyers.

In his usual brash manner, Doug marched directly up to Daniels and got in his face.

"You lie for your wife in the Bel Geddes murder?"

"We have nothing to say at this time," Jack Henley said with finality and pushed his way forward blocking for his client.

Doug pushed back.

"Mr. Daniels, how about a statement for the press? This is a chance to get your side of the story out before your wife—and maybe you—get crucified."

"We categorically and absolutely deny any involvement by Mr. Daniels or Dr. Norcroft in any crime. She is innocent of murder or conspiracy, and we are prepared to prove it. LAPD and the prosecutors have made a colossal mistake," Henley said curtly.

Doug could not get anything more out of the well-heeled couple, but his luck was still holding. Anson Burger came out of Central Booking and down the steps just after the

Daniels got into their car. Howard and Burger had a long history together. Howard had been more than fair in reporting about Burger's police practices and a couple of times over the years had defended him when the rest of the press were out for his blood during the recurring police scandals that periodically tarnished the reputation of the LAPD. As a result of Howard's reporting, Burger had been the only detective to walk away from the Rampart Division affair in the late 1990s, and he had credited Doug Howard's defense of him in the paper as the reason he was able to shake off the mud that sprayed on the whole division during the hearings.

"Anson, my friend, how about giving me the straight skinny on the Norcroft arrest."

"Hi, Doug. Not much to tell. Off the record?"

"Sure, but you have to drop me a crumb."

"A little tit for tat. I know the drill. Look, we had two persons of interest until yesterday."

"The Betty Boop wife and the Snow Queen?"

"Yes. And I've had a lot of pressure. You don't need to print that."

"I'm mum. So, why Dr. Norcroft?"

"She had the requirements: motive, means, and probably opportunity."

"Probably?"

"She has an alibi, but it doesn't look like it will hold up."

"If it does, do you have any hint of a murder for hire with Dr. Norcroft holding the purse strings?"

"Crossed my mind, but no evidence."

"Who's the DA?"

"Prentiss. He's sure this one is a career builder."

"And he'll find a way, or make one, as Seneca used to say."

"That's pretty much it."

"Thanks for the quotes. I have to call it in."

"Don't be too absolute. There's still an investigation under way."

"Not to worry."

Sybil was subjected to a Grand Jury inquiry which found the evidence sufficient to bind her over for trial. A week later, she was arraigned in Judge Able Randell's court and assigned to the "Hanging Judge" Lester Drammon for trial. Judge Randell would not permit bail, release on her own recognizance, or home detention with an ankle monitor. She changed her Guccis and Ralph Laurens for an orange jumpsuit and sneakers with no laces. Three months later, Sybil Norcroft, M.D., Ph.D., F.A.C.S. took the defendant's seat in Judge Drammon's courtroom. A month later, Voir dire was complete; and a jury of seven women and five men was impaneled along with twelve alternates, more evenly split by gender, race, and political choice.

Sybil appeared calm. Her face was placid and unrevealing. Her lawyers sat on either side of her, and her husband was seated on the row directly behind her. Everyone stood as Judge Drammon made his entry. He bade them sit, banged his gavel; and Sybil was on trial for her life. She was very well aware of that. Her lawyers assured her that acquittal was almost a certainty; but nonetheless, Sybil was acutely attune to the fact that this was not a civil case where the stakes had been money and reputation. This case could deprive her of her freedom for the rest of her life or result in her premature death. She had on sensible clothes and shoes; her hair was clean and shining, done up in a tight bun; and the only piece of jewelry she had on was a simple gold wedding band.

After the pro forma CSI, ME, trace lab, and detective testimony, which probably resulted in little positive attention being paid to the prosecution's argument or the defense's cross-examinations, interest in the trial picked up. Until Charles Daniels was called by the prosecution as a surprise witness, the other witness testimony was also a wash. It was, until then, becoming a yawner.

"Objection!" Jack Henley blurted out as he stood up and gesticulated.

"What grounds, Mr. Henley?" Judge Drammon asked.

"He's our witness, your honor!"

"He's on their list, Mr. Henley. Surely you are prepared to cross examine the man after the prosecution gets him on the record. Motion over-ruled."

The Senior Deputy District Attorney, Len Prentiss—a portly dandy in a $2,000 suit—continued his questions, "Mr. Daniels, where were you on the night of January 7th this year between the hours of ten and midnight?"

"At home in my bed."

"Alone?"

"No, I was with my wife—the defendant—sitting over there, by her attorney."

The judge said, "let the record show that the witness indicated the defendant, Ms. Norcroft."

"Were you with her the entire time? I mean in her physical presence?"

"No."

"No??!!"

There was a short pause while Prentiss worked to collect his thoughts in light of Daniel's unexpected response. This might just be too good to be true.

"And, Mr. Daniels, where was your wife and for how long when she was away from you?"

"She went to the toilet. I reckon the time when we were apart to be about three minutes."

He was perfectly deadpan when he let the wind out of Prentiss's sails. His weathered yachtsman's good looks were not lost on the women in the jury, and probably helped his wife.

There was another short pause for DA Prentiss to reconsider his change of approach of a moment ago.

"So, is it your testimony that Mrs. Daniels was home and in her bed for the entire time between ten and midnight?"

"Absolutely. We went to bed at nine, got better acquainted, watched TV until ten, then she went to sleep."

The women in the jury did not find it difficult to accept the image his statement painted.

"Did you go to sleep first or did she?"

"She did."

"Are you a sound sleeper, Mr. Daniels?"

"No. I have insomnia and have to take a sleep aid if I want to get some rest. I wake up several times a night even if I take one."

"Did you take a sleep aid that night, Sir?"

"No. I impose a strict schedule for taking them. That night and the next night were scheduled to be drug free."

"Do those drugs affect your memory, Mr. Daniels?"

"Not at all. I only take one, and it is a minor over-the-counter antihistamine called diphenhydramine. Its affects are quite minor and benign."

"Maybe you took one and slept deeply and it prevented you from remembering when your wife left the house to kill Mr. Bel Geddes."

Prentiss was on his feet, "Objection, your honor. That is outlandish and has absolutely no foundation in fact or evidence."

"Sustained. And, Mr. Prentiss, don't push your luck. Ladies and gentlemen of the jury, you are to disregard that question. Remember that the defendant is presumed innocent until and unless he or she is found guilty in a court such as this one by a jury such as the twelve of you."

"Mr. Daniels is it possible that you took a sleep aid, fell deeply asleep, and were unaware of whether or not your wife was by your side during the critical time period?"

"No, Sir. I am an absolute dictator for myself when it comes to taking medications. I keep assiduous records. I can produce them if it would help. My wife was in bed with me sound asleep until I fell asleep around one o'clock. I woke up three times to go to the bathroom; I have an enlarged prostate. She was asleep all the time. Each time I got up, it took me upwards of half an hour to get back to sleep; so, I have every confidence that Sybil was with me—in my physical presence—the entire night. Furthermore, we were together when we heard the news on KNX 1070 that Mr. Bel Geddes had been murdered. Sybil was absolutely dumbfounded. She could never be a poker player or an actress, Mr. Prentiss. She is simply unable to fake her emotions. She is as genuine as they get."

Prentiss could see that he was getting nowhere. It was like pounding sand down a rat hole; so, he said, "I'm done with this witness, your honor."

Jack Henley knew better than to queer things by asking more questions; so, he only asked two that would leave exactly the impression in the jurors' minds he wanted when Charles left the stand, "Mr. Daniels, is Sybil capable of murder?"

"No. She is a very rigid person about morals and the law. She is in complete control of her passions at almost all times. She has never committed a single violent act of which I am aware."

"Thank you. You know the penalty for perjury. Did you perjure yourself to protect your wife?"

"I did not."

Chapter Four

After a month of extensive travel, dyspeptic food in greasy spoons, and one night stays in cheap motels, the RH detectives finally hit some pay dirt in a miserable unincorporated little desert town called Pawrump, in Nye County, Nevada. The Dollar and a Half Pawn shop had a reputation of being an outlet for fences who acted as middlemen for thieves. A CI called RH detectives with what he called, a "red-hot tip worth big bucks."

"Yeah," Burger said, "what is your red-hot tip?"

"What's it worth?"

"Nothing until it pans out. I don't like being jacked around, and the LVPD and I are tight as Siamese twins. Now, what is it?"

"Not over the phone. I know the NSA and probably LVPD has all of the lines bugged. You gotta come to Pawrump, and I'll give you the best break you'll get in the crummy 'Super-Lawyer Murder.'"

"You can trust me. Anyway what's your name?"

"Runner, and do you think I just fell off the turnip truck? I ain't givin' you nuthin' 'till we look each other in the eyes. If you ain't interested, just fergit it. I'm hangin' up."

"Hold on Runner, don't get your knickers in a twist. We can work something out if you have good intel."

"We can work it out in Pawrump," Runner said with finality.

Burger sighed, "Listen, Runner, you sound like a valuable CI. I presume you're registered?"

"I got an official RCI certificate. It's framed and hangin' in my room."

"I'm going to go out on a limb. I'll meet you in Pawrump. This better be good. I am a good friend and a bad enemy, *capiche*?"

"Tommara at ten in front of the Dollar and a Half Pawn Shop. You know where it is?"

"No, but I have a GPS. I'll find it."

"It'll be worth your while. I *guarantee* it," Runner said emphasizing the word "guarantee." Bring cash. I'll tell you this, I seen somethin' in there worth the trip."

To Burger's surprise—and to the absolute astonishment of his new partner—Griselda Müller, better known as "Grizzly" which was more than just a play on her name—they walked into the pawn shop and found—prominently displayed—ten watches, a diamond tennis bracelet, and three gemstone rings that matched the description of the items stolen from the Bel Geddes residence on the night of the murder.

"Mr. Axelrod," Burger said, having learned the owner's name from LVPD criminal records, "we need to know where you got these items; who brought them in; and do you have more of them?"

"You got a warrant?" Axelrod said laconically with a well-practiced look of complete indifference.

"You wanna stay in business?" Grizzly asked showing her teeth. "We will be on you like ugly on a bear, and make your life hell for a year before you finally give up and move outta Dodge. You get my meaning? We got no time for your crap. All your records and all your info now; and we part friends; and you get to avoid being reported for being a fence."

Grizzly was persuasive. She was a solid, muscular woman with a battle-worn face. That helped.

"Okay, okay, no need to threaten. You kinda sorta jogged my memory, ya know. Seems some blond floozy wearin' last decade's high society clothes brought them in. Said she inherited them from her rich old gramma what she had cared for hand and foot for years. She didn't look like the carin'-for type, but who am I to judge, ya know? Name was…" He checked in his goods register… "Smiling Bright." He said it with a perfectly guileless face.

"Really," Burger said thoroughly pained. "And you accepted that?"

"WhommI to judge, man?" Axelrod said, affronted that he should be considered untrustworthy.

"Show us the rest of the merchandise, Mr. Axelrod, pronto!" Grizzly demanded.

Axelrod almost leaped and ran into the back room.

"Think he'll skip?" Grizzly asked Burger.

"Nah, he knows he's not in good enough shape. He wants to live another day and run this pitiful excuse for a business. He's doing exactly what you asked him to do."

Five minutes later, Axelrod returned and produced well over a million dollars-worth of genuine gold and gemstone jewelry and European watches.

"Think real hard about who brought you this stash," Burger said. "For starters, we'll have a sketch artist out here tomorrow am. Don't touch a drink of alcohol between now and then and get a good night's rest."

"That's offensive, officer; I don't drink. A while ago I took the lessons from the Mormon boys. Didn't quite take, I guess; but I have been thinkin' about becomin' a teetotaler ever since. You can count on me."

Axelrod and the sketch artist produced an image that looked something like Ann-Margaret Bel Geddes and a lot more like Dolly Parton or Marilyn Monroe. Axelrod insisted that the sketch include her very ample bosom, which was her outstanding characteristic. He made sure that the twin breast tattoos she sported of cupid shooting a sweet nymphet with a dart got prominent attention. He also thought there might have been another tattoo and something sort of strange about her hairdo, but he was not sure.

As it turned out, Ann-Margaret Bel Geddess was all too happy to show Grizzly her newly restructured breasts which were not marred by tattoos; so, that lead went nowhere. Anson and Grizzly set about looking for any evidence of involvement by the Daniels or of any other possible persons of interest they had interviewed.

They were just starting into that laborious undertaking and spreading the news over the cop internet sites when Sybil's private detectives, Drew Knox and Amber Littlefeather, learned from their own police internet surfing about the direction of the investigation. They were not hampered by legal restrictions or anything as inconsequential as moral fiber, and very shortly they were able to hack into Axelrod's and the LAPD's traffic. It was revealing. The most interesting finding was a cell phone call Axelrod made five minutes after the LAPD detectives left his establishment. It was to a cell phone belonging to a man named Henk van der

Hoef. Runner—the RCI whose real name was Theodore Maznick—gave them a valuable new direction to explore, and it did not occur to them to share their new information with the LAPD detectives, who treated PIs badly.

The trial was unexciting enough that, after the first four days of testimony, most of the news people just came by for an afternoon briefing. The only crime reporter who endured the entire trial and wrote a daily two paragraphs for the second page was Doug Howard from the *Times*. His perseverance would yield him an exclusive; but for now, he just plugged away satisfied to report on the mundane and unconvincing testimonies.

Sybil's outbursts were duly and fully talked about ad nauseum it seemed to Howard, but there was some sensational value given the defendant's high profile; so, he put as much as he could into print. No photos were allowed; so, Howard got the *Times* to spring for an artist. That added enough pizzazz to his pieces to keep him in print.

The defense case was no more exciting. Truth be known, there was little to be learned from actual facts divorced from feelings and opinions. Sybil Norcroft's life and her career were spotless, and she had no criminal record of any kind. She was a philanthropist, and a friend to the Latino, feminist, and LGBT communities. She was regarded as a political comer who was not interested in glory, politics, or partisan intrigues. She had enemies—almost entirely people whom she had had to correct during her stint as the chief of surgery, but also—including a few nurses who considered her abrasive. One nurse, Heather Larkin, RN, CNRN, had formally accused the distinguished doctor of having intentionally caused a patient's death by taking him off his ventilator. Nothing came of that.

Theodore Maznick [Runner]'s lead was to the Silver Dollar Saloon in downtown Las Vegas. He knew a guy who knew a guy who had a girl friend named Fancy—maybe not her real name—who worked there and also worked weekends in the Pawrump "Little Kittens Gentlemen's Club"—a legal brothel. Fancy had a neck tattoo of a very large but sweet black kitten with a white patch on its nose. She was also a suicide blond with three parallel bright purple stripes running from front to back on a white-girl 'fro. Drew Knox and Amber Littlefeather hoped against hope that she was the person who pawned Bel Geddes's jewelry. The two private eyes parked in the parking lot of the Viva Las Vegas Wedding Chapel on South Las Vegas Avenue near I-15. A Liberace theme wedding was just beginning when they settled down to wait for the action to pick up down the street. Their car would be significantly safer there than near Fancy's place of employment. They waited until a little after ten that night before they walked the four blocks—hands on gun butts—and pushed their way into the Silver Dollar Saloon. Business was booming. Amber was too short to see above the ocean of well coifed heads, and Drew was about to give up finding one blond floozy in a crowd of them.

"It's like looking for a needle in a needle-stack," he groused to his partner.

"We gotta try. I have a hunch that this will bring us closer to a real lead, and a bonus."

"In your dreams," muttered Drew.

"Stand on a chair; no one will notice," Amber said with a slightly wicked smile.

Drew knew it was true; so, as strange as it seemed to do so, he got up above the crowd. There she was, one elbow on the bar talking to a Hell's Angel drug smuggler. They both seemed to blend in perfectly with the rest of the crowd, with the exception of Drew and Amber. There was no mistaking that hair and that huge neck tattoo. It was better than a DNA match. He got down and whispered to Amber to go left, and he would go right and come up behind the biker.

Amber stepped up to their quarry and said, "Fancy?"

"Who wants to know?"

"This is a matter better discussed in private. Could we step outside for a minute?"

She let the handle of her gun show just a peep.

"Okay. What's this about?"

"Outside before I go deaf," Amber said and gave Fancy a friendly smile.

"Hey," the biker said as the two women moved away from him.

He reached out a powerfully muscled arm and put his huge hand on Fancy's arm. She pulled away with mild alarm. The biker reached again, then dropped to the floor when Drew stomped on the back of his knee. He started to raise a protest, and Drew rabbit punched the back of his neck. He slumped to the floor unconscious.

"Help, call 9-1-1. I think this guy just had a heart attack or a stroke or something," he shouted.

The scene became very busy, and Drew moved away and followed Amber and Fancy out the rear door and into the alley.

It was quiet, hot, and smelly in the alley. A rat scurried away from the dumpster.

"So, what's goin' on?" Fancy asked in a heavy Jersey accent.

Amber said, "You pawned some stolen jewelry in the Dollar and a Half Pawn Shop in Pawrump a while back."

Fancy looked like she was going to protest, but thought better of that idea when she saw the earnest expression on the private eye's face.

"And that jewelry came from a robbery homicide. You are in a heap of trouble, Fancy, like maybe goin' to HDSP [High Desert State Prison] for a very long time. We got you dead to rights. I'm gonna read you your rights."

"Hey, wait a minute. Just one minute. There must be something I can tell you that would help you, and you can help me. C'mon, you guys. What are you after that is more important than me?" she asked with a note of pleading in her voice.

"Did you kill the lawyer Bel Geddes?"

"Who? I didn't kill nobody. I don't know any lawyer Bel Geddes."

"Did you see somebody kill him?"

"No. I did not. I don't know nuthin' about no killin'."

"But, you did pawn the loot, Fancy, we got you on that. We better hear something good from you, or you're goin' down for murder one, maybe get the chair," Drew said with menace in his voice.

"Hey, they don't use the chair anymore. It ain't humane."

"Pardon me, Fancy; but I'm tellin' you, we learn something real important in the next five seconds or we'll see to it that you get the needle. That better?"

"Somehow, I don't feel much better. How 'bout I give up the one that give me the jewelry?"

"That'd be a good start," Amber said.

"It was a guy name of Henk van der Hoek, some sort of foreigner with an accent and all."

Coming from a woman with as thick of a Jersey accent as she had, it must have been a pretty heavy accent.

"How do we find him?"

"He lives in Palmdale, California in a trailer park, kind of a bad part of town," Fancy said.

"I'll just bet," Amber thought but did not say it out loud.

"We need more than that, like an address, e-mail, cell number, the whole Magillah."

"He's a pretty mean guy, ya know. You won't let him know it was me what put you on to him, will ya?"

"It's against our code of ethics. Your secret is safe with us, but don't leave town. In just a very few days, you are going to have to testify in a trial that is goin' on right now."

"Testify?"

"Yeah, as a witness, not a defendant."

That seemed to mollify her.

Chapter Five

"The defense calls Sybil Norcroft."

The courtroom was packed with excitement seekers, ghouls, and journalists of all stripes. It was leading up to the dramatic conclusion and the anticipated heavyweight champion fight between the beautiful and brilliant woman neurosurgeon and the lawyer for her dead career-long nemesis, the brilliant buffoon attorney.

Jack Henley led Sybil through a long and thorough description of her education, career, awards, and community activities. He threw her soft and slow ball questions to get her relationship with the murder victim out into the open and thereby to defuse the harsh cross-examination that was sure to follow.

After a full morning of what appeared to the people gathered in the courtroom gallery to be a series of paeans to Dr. Norcroft's magnificent career and model citizen life, Jack ended with what everyone in the courtroom was waiting to hear, "No more questions."

DA Prentiss rose from his chair with all of the majesty of his office. He was overweight, but carried it with style. Sybil had to exercise control not to stick her finger down her throat in a theatrical symbolic gesture. Prentiss walked up to within a foot of Sybil's face.

"Objection your honor, counsel is badgering the witness by entering her physical space."

"Sustained. Mr. Prentiss, step back three feet and don't approach the witness again without my permission," Judge Drammon said sharply.

Prentiss stepped back and fired a series of cross-examination questions that cast aspersion on every aspect of Sybil's education, training, marital, and social life, as well as upon her surgical skills.

"You hated the poor victim, Mr. Bel Geddes, didn't you, Ms. Norcroft?"

"Objection, it is Doctor Norcroft. She is a distinguished physician—a doctor of medicine—and should be accorded the courtesy of using her proper title."

"Sustained. I warned you once before, Mr. Prentiss. Let's do this right, and let's not need to have me instruct you again."

"Sorry, your honor. It won't happen again."

"Would you like me to repeat the question, *Dooctor*?"

"Yes."

"You hated the poor victim, Mr. Bel Geddess, did you not, Dr. Norcroft?"

"No."

"The members of the jury have heard days of testimony ad nauseum about how Mr. Bel Geddes tormented and picked on you and interfered in a myriad of ways with your career. It would not be surprising to hear that you disliked that."

"I did dislike that. But it was not personal. Mr. Bel Geddes exercised a strategy of annoying his opponents, causing them confusion and insecurity. I recognized that early on and did not pay attention to his antics."

"We'll leave that to the jurors to decide…Let's switch gears for a minute. Do you own expensive jewelry?"

"A few pieces."

"Did you not come into possession of a few more, rather extremely valuable pieces of jewelry in the recent past month or so, Doctor?"

The question surprised Sybil a little, but she should have anticipated it and prepared; but it was easy to answer, whatever Prentiss's intentions were.

"No."

"No Rolexes, diamond baseball bracelets, diamond pendants, or gold rings, and necklaces?"

"No."

"Would it surprise you to learn that a pawn shop owner in Pawrump, Nevada tentatively identified you as having pawned several very expensive pieces of jewelry with him shortly after the murder of Mr. Bel Geddes? Rather a telling coincidence, don't you think?"

"Objection, lacks foundation," Henley said.

"I'll allow some latitude here; but, Mr. Prentiss, you will need to put some legs under that line of questions if you intend to pursue it further."

"Thank you, your honor. Now, Dr. Norcroft, you may answer my question."

"I don't know where Pawrump, Nevada is. I have never been inside a pawn shop in my entire life. I did not steal any jewelry, let alone any from Mr. Bel Geddes. I did not fence any jewelry, and I did not receive an iota of material benefit from the death of Mr. Bel Geddes. I presume you have been through every item in my financial life in the past month, and I defy you to point to a single suspicious item."

Henley had tried to interrupt her, but Sybil was speaking loudly and rapidly; and she was on a roll.

"We'll come back to that, especially the part about you not obtaining gain from the death of Mr. Bel Geddes. But for now, I have a different question. Do you own a shot gun?"

"No. My husband owned one about ten years ago, but he gave it away in a charitable auction."

"Have you ever fired a shotgun?"

"No, you searched my house and examined me and all of my clothing. Did you find any evidence of gunshot residue, Mr. Prentiss?"

The judge interrupted, "Dr. Norcroft, the attorney will ask the questions; and you will answer them. That's how it works in this court."

"Thank you, your honor. I was just trying to be sure that the truth, the whole truth, and nothing but the truth comes out in the trial."

"Dr. Norcroft, careful. You are treading on dangerous ground. Your outburst was close to contempt of court. Do it again, and I will cite you."

Sybil looked steadily at the judge. It was a little disconcerting.

"Proceed, Mr. Prentiss."

"Did you hate Paul Bel Geddes, the unfortunate victim of someone's hatred?"

"Asked and answered, No."

"Did you hire a hitman?"

"Certainly not. I wouldn't have the first idea about to how to go about such a thing."

"Did you conspire with anyone else to have Mr. Bel Geddes murdered?"

"Certainly not."

"Hummh, we should explore that a bit. Do you have several very dedicated servants, Dr. Norcroft?"

"This is the American West, Mr. Prentiss. Nobody has servants; no self-respecting Westerner would ever consider himself or herself to be a servant. I do not have servants—dedicated or otherwise."

"Surely, you are aware that many Hollywood celebrities and rich people—such as you and your husband—have servants."

"And I am aware that Mr. Bel Geddes and other rich attorneys have outright servants whom they exploit. I even know that you, Sir—a rich attorney—have servants."

"I see no reason for you to lump me with your obvious disdain for attorneys. It is unfair, and I am offended."

"If the shoe fits, Attorney Prentiss."

"I warned you, Dr. Norcroft. Your contentious insults are duly noted, and I hereby cite you for contempt of court. The fine will be $500 and you will spend five days in jail. Perhaps that will help you to reconsider your contempt of this court," Judge Drammon said angrily.

"That would not be half the value of the contempt I feel, Judge," Sybil responded, ignoring her attorney, Jack Henley's, restraining hand waving from the defendant's table.

"Make it $1000 and a week," the judge said and glared.

"Not even close."

"$5,000 and a week. I would make the jail time longer, but we have to get through this long drawn-out trial. Now, Mr. Henley, caution your client to control her mouth, and we will proceed. Mr. Prentiss, I would favorably entertain a motion for you to treat this defendant as a hostile witness."

"So requested."

"Granted, proceed."

Sybil was boiling, but worked to get herself calmed down. Prentiss was flustered and put off course by the hostile exchange and had to pause for several minutes to find his place on his yellow legal pad pre-trial preparation notes.

"Ah, yes," he said, "is not true that you employ a number of illegal immigrants as servants on your ranch and in your home?"

"It is not true."

"Are you acquainted with Jose and Maria Innocenta Pomposo-Alvarez, Donita Pomposo, Pancho and Carlita Rodriguez, and Marcos and Viviana Hernandez?"

"I certainly am."

"Ah, ha. Then you admit to having lied to the court on a substantive issue, do you not, Dr. Norcroft?"

"Again, I do not. Have you any interest in objective and verifiable facts, or do you just want to flail around in misinformation and half-truths or outright lies?"

"Remember, Doctor, the attorney asks; you answer—not the other way around," the judge remonstrated one more time.

"Sorry, your honor, no offense meant. But I keep slipping into that governing rule of my life and my profession where unvarnished and unembroidered truth is a paramount."

Henley and Prentiss sighed together.

"Let's move forward. In fact, let's get through this area pretty quickly, preferably before the lunch break," Judge Drammon said, his patience nearly exhausted.

"So, Doctor, please explain to me where I might be mistaken in the matter of your having very dedicated servants who would be willing to do just about anything for you."

"That is a far stretch from your original question, but here is some truth. Everyone you named is a permanent resident of the United States and is a holder of what is known as a "Green Card." They all obtained that status by virtue of their long-term stable and gainful employment. In fact, they are no longer employees, although early on they were. And they were never servants. They are, in fact—as a group—49% owner/partners in my horse breeding agri-business. They are also, in fact, my friends. We have a relationship of mutual respect."

"That can be subject to verification through the USCIS, Dr. Norcroft. Be mindful of the laws against perjury."

"If it is permitted, I have photocopies of all of the documentation for my partners, Counselor. Further, I have a copy of their Green Cards and the official USCIS letter welcoming them into the country. For your convenience, I also have the telephone number of the local government office. I am sure you can verify everything I have told you with a quick telephone call before the lunch break."

"I will do just that. But we are being sidetracked. The status of your…partners…is not the issue. My questions center on how much they would be willing to do to repay you for your kindness and honesty in working for them. They each praise you to the heavens."

"That's very nice of them. What has that got to do with this murder trial?"

"Could be everything. I'll get to the heart of it."

"That would be refreshing."

"Tsk, tsk, Dr. Norcroft," the judge said exasperated but unwilling to get into another exchange with the formidable woman.

Sybil nodded as a small note of contrition.

"Did you ask your…partners…to kill Mr. Bel Geddes?"

Sybil laughed out loud.

The judge flashed her a look.

"Sorry, it was just so ridiculous that it seemed like a joke. My answer is a simple and emphatic, 'no'! It is an insult, and I think a racist one at that to make such an accusation."

"I did not mean any type of racial profiling…" Prentiss started then stopped himself realizing that this overly bright woman was drawing him in again, and he was losing control of the questioning.

"Could they have done it on their own out of a misguided sense of loyalty and gratitude to you?"

"No, again. But you can ask them. They are reliable members of the society."

"They are on my witness list, Madam," Prentiss said. "We'll see what truth there really is. I have no further questions for now, but I reserve the right to recall her if the need arises."

"I won't be going anywhere," Sybil said to get the last word in.

There was a ripple of laughter from the jury and the courtroom spectators.

Judge Drammon banged his gavel. The reporters made a bee-line to their phones and computers. The exchange between the judge, the prosecutor, and the feisty witness was great stuff. Doug Howard skewed his article towards the idea that the testimony was a victory for feminism.

Chapter Six

Lt. Anson Burger met or had telephonic or electronic communication with his task force of five detectives, a full time secretary, and a computer and electronics expert. After two weeks, they had narrowed their field to 982 possibles based on history of negative interaction with Bel Geddes. This included disgruntled employees—46 possibilities there—angry plaintiffs who lost to the unpopular attorney in court or settlement procedures—886 possibilities—a good random sample of people whom he had sued for personal reasons and usually whose lives were ruined—12 of those—and a smaller number, but a very vehement group who had been clients of Bel Geddes in losing cases. The complaint for all of those people was that their attorney had strung them out for months—even years—before unceremoniously dumping them without a decent explanation. That number was a more manageable 15 people. Finally, there were 23 people who had expressed opinions in print objecting to him—and often all lawyers—in the form of letters to the editor, blogs, e-mails, and complaints to various courts and attorney organizations. They did not seem all that angry or rational; so, Burger decided to let them slide for the time being.

He did not like Detective Third Class Max Broom or Sergeant Clement Ashley; so, he assigned them to the massive 886 set of possibles. They each got an assistant. Acting on a hunch—a detective's gut feeling—he decided to team up with Detective Adrienne MacInnerneny to rule out the involvement of the 15 disgruntled former clients. In what was possibly a bit of serendipity, MacInnerneny found a name that rang a bell in one of the first three folders she was assigned. The name of van der Hoef caught her eye, and she wrestled with her memory of the murder book notes for where that name had come up.

"Burger, does the name 'van der Hoef' mean anything to you?"

"Yeah, it does. Actually, I have been kind of hunting for the guy. In Nevada, we got a clue that the pawn broker where we found Bel Geddes's stolen jewelry phoned a guy by that name just after we talked to him. Lemme think. I have his first name on the tip of my tongue…Oh, yeah, it's Henk. Henk van der Hoef."

MacInnerneny said, "That seems like a lead that has at least two avenues leading to the man. Maybe we ought to follow our guts and at least put in some gumshoe time to find the man and have a chat."

"Might as well, can't hurt. Let's get on the computers and let VICAP, the LAPD files, and the prison records give us a hand. I neglected to ask, why did you ask about him?"

"I didn't even know it was a him. I just found a very short note that somebody with that last name wrote a complaining note to the chief judge, to the LA bar, and to a "Victims of Lawyers" help group. There were no details."

"You work on that angle, and I'll see if I can get an address or some kind of a 10-20."

Private Eyes Drew Knox and Amber Littlefeather had a devil of a time locating their only real lead, Henk van der Hoef; but they were ahead of the regular police detectives. They had a name and a general location of California, but not much else He had no criminal record; and aside from being a member of the Maritime Construction Union, he did not have any associations with groups, churches, humanitarian groups, hunting clubs, sports outfits, or anything else. He had no known associates or girl-friends. He had no presence in the social media. There was a small piece of information on the internet that listed him as a one-time employee of the Westminister County Boatyards where he helped build PT boats for the navy. He had no land-line phone, and no known address. He was enough of a cipher that Knox and Littlefeather began to worry that he might be dead.

Their search led them to the name of a possible relative, one Gerrit van der Hoef, who also once worked for the Westminister County Boatyards. That surely was not a coincidence; so, the PIs made a beeline for Westminister County to seek help from the local gendarmerie to find Gerrit even if they could not find Henk.

The company gave them a last known address for Gerrit, but had lost all contact with Henk. They did verify that the two men were brothers. Both of them had reputations for being contentious, but no history of violence that the company knew about. Police records were similarly unrevealing, although Henk had a record of two fights in five years with union stewards. Gerrit had had a complaint sworn out against him by a doctor's office employee. Interest began to increase when they learned that the doctor in question was none other than Sybil Norcroft—the society brain surgeon—who was already on trial for Bel Geddes's murder. They found Gerrit in his trailer house in Palmdale, the town next to Lancaster, in the high desert north of Los Angeles.

Drew and Amber stopped their company car in front of the trailer which was the last known address for Gerrit. He surveyed the trailer park with an experienced eye.

"Tell me what you see, Amber," he said after he was done thinking.

"SOS. Looks like the usual trailer trash—people, buildings, lots, and cars. One bit of difference is that Gerrit's place seems to have been cleaned up recently. He has a new paint job, and looks like he just got a new used Ford pick-up—still has the dealer paper plates. Otherwise, not much that helps, it seems to me."

"What do you make of what you see?"

Amber took a turn to think and to scrutinize the scene more carefully.

"Ah, boss, Gerrit seems to have come into a bit of money lately, maybe quite a bit. Maybe we've been looking for the wrong brother."

Drew and Amber walked briskly up to van der Hoef's trailer home door and knocked. They were well aware of a dozen pairs of eyes following them.

"Whadda you want? Didn't ya see the no solicitin' sign and the bad dog sign. Git off my porch or I'll sic my pit bull on ya."

"We're not solicitors," Drew said

"Heard that before. It's that or the J Dubs or the Mormons. I'm tellin' ya for the last time, whatever you're sellin or preachin, I'm too broke to buy anythin'. I know who I'm gonna vote for—which is nobody—and I've already found

Jesus. So, if you aren't bringin' me free beer or a Publishers Clearing House Sweepstakes cutie carryin' a letter guaranteein' me seven thou a week, I ain't interested; so git out."

"Nice guy", Amber said. "Let me try."

"Have at it, Pard."

"Mr. van der Hoek, we are private investigators. We need some information on how to contact your brother, Henk. We are investigating a possible inheritance he might get. We have to find him first, then be sure that he's the right guy."

"You for real?"

"Cross my heart and hope to die."

They heard four separate locks open, and van der Hoek let them in.

"So, what's the straight skinny about this inheritance? Nobody in our family ever had two nickels to rub together."

"We'll get farther faster if you'll just let us ask the questions. Then, we'll be out of your hair as soon as possible."

The two private detectives looked around the trailer. There was a new TV, a new bed set that was not even out of the store wrapping, and the trailer's shelves were lined with dozens of boxes of canned food. The man himself was dressed in expensive Yuppie clothes that seemed out of place in amongst the trailer trash. His Cole Hahn shoes were new and shiny. They exchanged looks and tucked away the images for future reference.

"Let's get right down to it. First, is it true that you have a brother named Henk?"

"Yeah, so what?"

"Do you have a current address for him, Mr. van der Hoef?"

"Maybe."

"Really, 'maybe'? How about making this easy. We don't want to take anything from you. We don't have anything to sell, and we're not cops. We just need to talk to the man. It could be a good thing for the family. By the way, just for the sake of interest, are the two of you on good terms?"

"Yeah, we are. So, okay, I guess you gotta trust somebody. You seem pretty harmless. Here's his address. And I got a telephone number and e-mail if ya want it."

He wrote the information down on a new memo sheet and handed it to Drew.

"Thanks," Drew said.

"It's nuthin'", Gerrit said.

"Well, we'll be on our way, Mr. van der Hoef. Oh, please don't call Henk, we want to sort of surprise him, you know."

"Sure."

"If they are the least bit close, Henk's phone is ringing right now," Amber said as they got into their car.

"It's about an hour or an hour and a half to Cucamonga at this time of day. Let's boogie," Drew said and broke speed limits all the way which kept them up with the rest of the traffic and out of the interest of cops.

Henk lived in a small neat rambler in Rancho Cucamonga in what was obviously a fairly new subdivision of the city. Several houses were still under construction, and very few of the homes had finished their landscaping. Henk's place still had the realtor sign up with a "SOLD" sign glued to the company's advertisement.

They knocked on the door three times.

"I see movement. He's in there," Amber said.

They tried again. No response. They could hear the TV blaring—a baseball game.

"I'm going around to the back; see if I can rouse him. If we make a fuss out front here, we'll have the neighbors reporting us," Drew said to Amber.

He knocked on the back door three loud raps.

"Get your donkey off my proppity. No salesmen. No nothin'. Git off or I'll blow you off."

Drew saw a well-dressed scowling blond man through the kitchen door window. He was holding a shot gun.

"No need for any trouble," Drew said and backed away one step.

The door flung open, and Henk van der Hoef stepped out far enough to fire one round in the general direction of Drew.

"Now do ya git the idea?" Henk snarled. "Come here again and I'll sic the dogs on ya or call the cops. You ain't welcome. Git!"

Drew got and did it double time.

"What just happened?" Amber asked.

"A police incident. Let's call the local cops. Maybe they can get something out of nice Mr. van der Hoef. It's not worth being perforated full of buck shot holes."

They had a talk with a Rancho Cucamonga desk sergeant. After they finished their discussion, including the interest on the part of LAPD detectives in a murder case that was in progress right then, the sergeant made a call to the Chief of D's office and was quickly routed to Detective Griselda (Grizzly) Müller.

"This is Sergeant Ray Duggins, RCPD. I think we have something for you in your investigation concerning the Bel Geddes murder. Hope it's not too late. I understand the trial is beginning to wind down. Anyways, I got a couple private dicks who had a run-in this afternoon. Might be related."

"Put them on, please," Grizzly asked.

Drew told the LAPD detective the short form of he and Amber's investigation, including the violence by shotgun that had occurred.

"There was no need for such hostility, and I think it could be more than a coincidence that a shotgun was used. Maybe your task force could make a pass at this guy. My partner and I have started to think that there may be more to this case than just what's coming out in that LA courtroom."

"Maybe. Thanks for the tip. We aren't getting much but holes in our shoes and tired butts; so we haven't got anything to lose. We'll keep you posted. You two will need to give a formal statement and maybe even have to testify. If there is something to all of this, we need to have your notes, photos, whatever; and we will want you to stay clear of the investigation. Okay?"

"Yes. You get the big bucks. It's not worth us getting shot. We'll report to you and to our clients and will just wait to hear from you. Please do us the courtesy of a heads-up when you get something."

"Thanks for getting right to us," Grizzly said, "we'll keep you in the loop."

Detectives Burger and Müller decided to play it safe. They weren't all that keen on being shot at either. Burger got back to Sergeant Duggins and requested a SWAT team from RCPD to go with them to the van der Hoef residence. They waited until late evening. It was a moonless dark night, perfect for the execution of the no-knock warrant. The cavalry gathered outside both entrances into Henk van der Hoek's house. The SWAT captain spoke quietly into his shoulder-mic.

"On my count of five, everybody in. Copy?"

"Copy," came the reply from the troops in front and back.

"Okay, one, two, three…"

Chapter Seven

S enior Deputy DA Len Prentiss resumed his interrogation of Sybil Norcroft after a two hour recess for lunch.

"We're going to look into some other things in your history, Dr. Norcroft. You should be informed that you can invoke the protections of the Fifth Amendment to the Constitution if you decide it is in your best interests any time during this questioning. Do you understand your rights?"

"Yes."

"Do you want to proceed?"

"Yes, let's get it over with. I have nothing to hide."

"Do you know a doctor named Darryl Hankin, the ENT specialist who testified here earlier in this trial?"

"I do."

"And do you know Heather Larkin RN, CNRN personally? She also gave testimony here. Do you recall those two testimonies or will it be necessary for me to have their transcripts read back to you?"

"I remember what seem to me to be the important aspects of their testimonies."

"Dr. Hankin stated for the record that there were several occasions when you threatened him over what you considered inappropriate advances but were, in reality, only attempts to be friendly. He also stated that you spoke frequently of your animosity towards a certain lawyer whom you considered to be harassing you. Does that jibe with your memory of the testimony of Dr. Hankin?"

"Yes."

"Please respond to his allegations."

"It would be a gross understatement to say that Dr. Hankin does not like me and considers me to be a threat to his practice. Specifically, I do the entirety of an operation called a transsphenoidal hypophysectomy—including the approach through the nose—which he considers to be the exclusive territory of ENT surgeons. In addition, on many occasions, he has been sexually inappropriate—both in terms of verbalizations and unwanted touching. I challenged him on that in public, and more than once. He swore to get even, and here he is in court getting even. The short answer is that his testimony was at best skewed by his animosity, and more accurately full of misstatements and outright lies."

"What about nurse Larkin? Does she have an axe to grind as well? It seems that you have created more than your share of serious enemies. Can't always be that you are perfectly correct and professional, and all of the rest are jealous and vindictive, can it?"

"You have only brought two people here to be witnesses. It is not exactly fair to be so selective about establishing what you want to have the jury know about my personality and character. Now, as to Heather Larkin. She is a born-again Christian who thinks that the woman's place is in the home submitting to her husband. She takes great personal umbrage in the fact that I am a very active and prominent feminist and have held national offices in feminist organizations. I am something of a celebrity in LGBT circles, and that offends her ideology based on the Judeo-Christian Bible. She developed a severe anger, even hatred, when she decided that I had purposely assisted in the death of a patient by taking him off life supports for my personal gain. All of that was duly investigated and ascertained to be entirely erroneous. She vowed to see me get my comeuppance if it was the last thing she ever did.

"Nurse Larkin took every occasion possible to tarnish my reputation and to impugn my character. None of it stuck. She is a bitter woman who—during this trial—allowed her personal animus to cloud her judgment. I will be blunt. She lied. And she did so for purely vengeful reasons. I did not make the statements she attributed to me either in private or in public. I never threatened Mr. Bel Geddes; and Dr. Henkin and Ms. Larkin's statements under oath are inaccurate, even prevarications."

Sybil's delivery was practiced, and she gave her testimony in a calm and professional manner devoid of anger or other emotion. She saw mixed indications of belief and disbelief in the jurors' faces.

Prentiss took Sybil through similar questions about the testimony of her secretary and the people at the New Year's party who heard her make overheated outbursts. She thought she handled the difficult questioning fairly well. She was very tired and very much relieved when court was adjourned for the evening.

"How do you think it's going?" she asked Jack Henley.

"Pretty well," he said. "I think you did well, but there are three or four jurors who seem to be leaning towards the prosecution. I tell you, Sybil, I wish we had some more evidence—something that would nail down reasonable doubt."

Chapter Eight

The RCPD SWAT captain finished his count "…four, five." The front and rear doors shattered from the SWAT battering rams. Noise from two dozen cops, two brilliant flash bangs, and an impenetrable cloud of smoke filled the first floor of the new house. The sole occupant screamed and huddled on the floor. He was not nearly the fire-breather who had faced down the two private detectives earlier in the day. Lt. Burger rode in the ambulance to the San Antonio Community Hospital on Milliken Avenue in Rancho Cucamonga with Henk van der Hoef. Although the thoroughly cowed Dutchman probably did not need restraints, Burger kept handcuffs on him for the entire ambulance ride and during his stay in the ER. That stay was brief; the only thing wrong with him was a pair of ringing ears and slowly improving snow blindness.

Burger and Grizzly drove Henk to Parker Center and ungently sat him down on a hard metal chair with his hands and feet cuffed to steel rings on the table and the floor.

"Time to talk, Henk. You don't mind if I call you Henk, do you?"

"It's my name, ain't it?"

"Well, Henk, as we say out here in the West, you are in a heap of trouble. First of all you took a shot at two citizens just going about their work. That's attempted murder. And it gets worse. We did a little look-around in your house. Guess what we found?"

"I give up. Is this some kind of a stupid game?"

"No game. No, Sir, nothing fun or funny here. We found a pawn ticket from the Pawrump, Nye County, Nevada Dollar and a Half Pawn shop. Signed by a Mr. Axelrod. Any of that ring a bell, Henk?"

"Maybe, what of it?"

"There's a bit more. We looked around in some kinda hidden drawers in your new place. We found some fancy lady's jewelry there. Now, you don't look like the type to wear such expensive and feminine bling; so, we did a little investigating. Lo, and behold, we found out that all of that jewelry was stolen. Am I getting through to you, Henk?"

"Whatta you want outta me?"

"Before I share that with you, I have one more thing to let you know about. It seems that the jewelry was part of a major heist during a murder—a particularly nasty murder. I'm about to ask you a couple of more questions, but every question it takes to get to the full truth is going to go against you when I make my recommendations to the DA. So, anything you want to tell me?"

"Maybe, I oughta get a lawyer."

"Maybe so, but as soon as you do, we can't make any offers. You know that, right?"

"I guess so," Henk said, a little less confidently.

"How did you get that jewelry? Don't waste my time with denials. We have you cold on personal possession and for selling the stolen goods. At the very least we have you on felony murder."

"What's that? I thought murder was a felony period."

"It's when a death occurs during the commission of a felony. See, even if you were just driving the getaway car when a crime took place where somebody died—even the criminal—you are as guilty as the killer. Now, maybe you did the killing. Maybe you just came by and found the door open, the guy dead and stole his stuff. Maybe you were contacted by the killer and fenced his stuff which would not be as serious. See where this might be going, Henk?"

"Kinda. So if I maybe could give you information, what's in it for me?"

"Let's get real. It depends on the quality, importance, and accuracy of your information. It also depends on the timeliness. There is a trial going on right now, and it is possible that an innocent person could get the death penalty just because you withheld information. I guess you could get a good word from us; or you could get a reduced sentence; or you might get probation; it is even possible that you could get time served for while you were hanging around in jail waiting for the law to take its course. If your information were to be good enough, I guess you could get immunity."

"If I could give you the killer, how about I get full immunity. If that ain't so, then I ain't interested. I got an almost clean record, and I want it to stay that way."

"We got great circumstantial evidence on you. Frankly, I like you for this. You have a history of violence and B&Es, and you have the loot. Why should we look for some other dude?"

"You tryin' to bluff me?"

"I don't play poker, too busy. You have five seconds before I leave, and you go out in cuffs to be booked for capital murder. *Capiche?*"

"Okay, okay. I got somethin', but you can't let it get out who told you. I get full immunity because I can take you to the killer and because I can finger him and testify in court. I am innocent, and I know who the guilty guy is."

"You got my attention, Henk. Don't let me stop you from talking as much as you want," said Burger.

The trial of Sybil Norcroft resumed the next morning.

"You are still under oath, Dr. Norcroft," Judge Drammon said, looking better rested and less exasperated.

Sybil nodded.

"You may continue, Mr. Prentiss," the judge ordered.

"Thank you, your honor. Dr. Norcroft, I'll be entirely candid, I do not believe in your alibi. Under some twist of spousal privilege, you and your husband are hiding the fact that you had opportunity—time—to got to Mr. Bel Geddes's house, kill him, steal his jewelry, and get back home unobtrusively enough to fake an alibi. I ask you, in accordance with your oath—hand on the Bible, and before God—did you murder Paul Devon Bel Geddes? Bear in mind that opening up to all of us here will bring you a measure of peace. You can do the right thing here and now."

"You must have asked me that twenty times, Mr. Prentiss. The answer is the same: I did not kill Paul Bel Geddes. I did not steal from him."

"You certainly benefited from his death. The law suit has been cancelled. You won without a fight."

"His partners—acting on advice from the local chapter of the American Trial Lawyers Association—were persuaded that the case had no merit. No one else has stepped up to carry on with the suit. It was such a bad case, that I never feared losing it. It was annoying, nothing more. Certainly not enough to kill over. You have a lousy case against me, and you are desperate. That is the long and short of it. Give it up. I am not just not guilty; I am innocent."

Sybil spoke with passion and firm conviction which she conveyed to the jurors with all the strength she had.

"I have no further questions for this witness," Prentiss said, hoping to keep the sigh out of his voice.

"Look, I admit I got hold of some of the jewelry from that lawyer's place," van der Hoef said. "But I never had nothin' to do with his death.

"C'mon, Henk, you're wasting our time."

"This is a tough one. You have no idea how tough."

"Tell us. Get it off your chest. It'll do you good," Grizzly said, speaking up for the first time during the questioning.

"Oh, man. Maybe I'll go to hell for telling you this. But it ain't right for me to take the fall. What happened was this, my brother hated this Bel Geddes guy with a passion like you never seen before. He got jacked around for eleven years, eleven years! by that putz. He had tons of pain, and he had a good case against the doctor."

"What doctor?" Grizzly asked.

"The one's on trial...what's her name?...Norcroft. She wouldn't operate on Gerrit, wouldn't write him a letter to be able to retire on disability; and she fought against him until Bel Geddes dropped out of the suit. That schmuck attorney never done a thing to defend Gerrit...just shined him on and neglected him for the whole eleven years. When Gerrit learned about the suit bein' dropped in the newspaper, he went all postal. But he could never get hold of either that femmanazi doctor or that crooked hack of a lawyer. What he done, was started to drink like a fish. He lost his job. His wife left him, and he had to live on what little he could get from knockin' over Seven Elevens and such. Startin' last year, he got hooked on meth.

"Then one day, he come over to my old place in Compton and told me that he came into some real money. He had a bunch of diamonds, some big enough to choke ya if ya accidently swallowed one. He wanted my help to get rid of 'em, and said I could share half and half on account of we was brothers. He kept pesterin' me, and he was so crazy over the whole thing that I finally broke down and agreed to help. I knew this creepy dude in Nevada—done a bit of business with him before. I gave him—name's Axelrod—a call. He told me I had to go up to Nevada and bring the stuff with me.

"He was a pretty good guy, give me a decent price considerin' the circumstances. I kept some of the ice; Gerrit said I could; but I didn't dare try and sell it. Too much publicity. Too many cops."

"You're doin' good, Henk," Burger said. "You're on a roll, and my partner and I are listening real close now. Don't quit while you're ahead."

"Am I ahead? I ain't heard the word 'immunity' yet? I ain't goin' ta say nothin' more until I do."

"Where can we find Gerrit?" Burger asked.

Henk ran his fingers over his lips in a sewing motion.

Twenty questions later, he still would not budge from his tactic of silence.

"Tell you what we'll do, Henk. You lead us to Gerrit; and he gets convicted and gets a sentence that holds up, you get your immunity."

"Sounded like a lot of ifs," Henk said.

"Just reasonable guarantees that what you are telling us is the truth. You understand, we can't get you immunity and then get egg on our face."

"That'd sure be a rotten run of luck," Henk said angrily. "But, without immunity, you'll never find Gerrit in a thousand years. He's like a weasel. He is hidin' in a perfect place with the perfect disguise. He will get away and live on the money he got from the diamonds, and he'll laugh at you for the rest of his life."

"All right, Henk. Can we walk there, go by car, or do we have to fly? You have your immunity signed, sealed, and delivered as soon as we arrest him, and he gets to court. That suit you?"

"I guess."

They loaded up in the detectives' car. Henk would not tell the detectives a thing beyond, "turn here, turn there, and go another ten miles and turn left. I tell you more when you do that."

It was exasperating, but it soon became apparent that they were headed north on Highway 14 towards the high desert. They drove into a visitors' parking lot in a rundown trailer park in Palmdale, the palms being a misnomer originating from the early Mormon settlers who thought the thousands of Joshua Trees were palm trees. It was hot and dusty. It is hot and dusty in Palmdale eight months of the year and then it is windy and cold.

"I ain't getting' out of the car," Henk said. "I can't have my own brother know I ratted on him."

Burger cuffed him to the steel rings attached to the roll bar arching over the back seat and locked the doors.

"Stay put."

Henk shrugged in acknowledgment of the futility of trying to escape. He got as far down in the seat as he could.

Burger and Griselda Müller walked as nonchalantly as they could to about forty feet from the trailer.

"Go around to the back. I don't want him to have a chance to run," Burger told his junior partner.

He walked up to the door and banged on it.

"Police," he barked in his deep baritone voice.

He did it twice more then kicked in the door. The place was clean as the proverbial whistle. There was not a sign of Gerrit van der Hoef or that he had ever been there.

He opened the back door, and said "clear" to Grizzly who hardly needed words since she could see it written in his face.

They tossed the place as thoroughly and destructively as they could; but he had obviously been warned off, if in fact he had ever been there. They questioned the neighbors, most of whom were not forthcoming, and the trailer supervisor who was. Indeed, Gerrit had lived there for almost three years. But about a week ago, he just lit out. Did not pay his last month's rent.

"He wasn't there," Burger said to Henk. "You jerkin' us around, punk? It's no deal on the immunity if you don't come through for us."

"I know where he'd go. I swear."

"Take us."

"Take off the cuffs. My arm's killin' me. I'll give you directions all the way."

They ended up in another trailer park, this time in the shanty sections around the China Lake Naval Air Station. It was more run down than the trailer trash city in Palmdale. The trailer in question had obviously been abandoned some time ago.

This time Grizzly banged on the rickety front door almost knocking it off its rusty hinges. Burger took his turn going around the back.

Grizzly knocked down the door and jumped into the trash ridden wreck with her gun out. She heard a side window bang open, and when her eyes adjusted to the dark, she saw a foot disappear out the opening.

She ran outside and yelled, "Hey Burger, he rabbitted. He's headed north towards the water tank."

She set out on hot pursuit. Burger fell over a rusty oil can and landed on a smashed up motorcycle getting two nasty rust laden cuts which slowed him down and doubled his vocabulary of obscenities and profanity. He was well behind his partner when he heard a gun-shot; specifically, the unmistakable sound of 12 gauge shotgun.

Chapter Nine

Deputy DA Prentiss started his summation for the prosecution with an apology, "Ladies and gentlemen of the jury. I appreciate that you have spent a long and tedious time here as the trial has unfolded. I plan to convince you, if you are not already sure that this woman—the doctor over there—is guilty of murder. It will take some time, maybe all morning for me to lay it all out in a logical order for you. Bear with me. You want to do the right thing, and I will help you to do it.

"The animosity between the defendant—that's the blond woman in the beige dress sitting with her lawyer at the defendant's table—and Mr. Paul Devon Bel Geddes—who is not here—has been in progress for more than a decade. I must speak for him, since I speak for the people. Mr. Bel Geddes was murdered, and we are to present compelling evidence of what led up to his death and who was the murderer.

"Their first encounter came when a promising young man from a prominent family—Brendan McNeely—underwent a major neurosurgical operation under the hands of Sybil

Norcroft, the defendant. The boy died in surgery, and Ms. Norcroft was sued by his grieving family for medical malpractice. Because of his sterling reputation in the medical malpractice field, the family sought the services of Mr. Bel Geddes. That was the first of many such suits; it seems that the neurosurgeon who is being tried here for murder has run afoul of the standards of practice on many occasions, and Mr. Bel Geddes had to step in to set things right."

Sybil passed a note to Jack Haney, "Object. He is mischaracterizing all of the suits—I won almost all of them."

Jack gave a very small negative shake of his head. It is almost unheard of for an opposing attorney to interrupt his opponent's summation.

Over the course of the next three and a half hours and extending into the lunch hour, Prentiss went over the history of the malpractice suits—always omitting who won or lost—and the accumulated circumstantial evidence against Sybil. During the presentation of the malpractice cases, Prentiss paid particular attention to the McNeely case and dwelled on the testimony of Heather Larkin CNRN who had protested that Dr. Norcroft had discontinued life-supports prematurely and, in effect, murdered the young man. He duly presented—in a brief rapid-fire overview—that the hospital had cleared Dr. Norcroft of any wrongdoing. He emphasized the callous nature of the famous "Snow Queen's" manner in dealing with supposedly brain dead patients.

He also emphasized the testimony of several of Sybil's front office girls—and let the jury know that the arrogant doctor often referred to them as the FROGs—regarding a very prolonged suit involving a workman named Gerrit van der Hoef. One of the girls told of a semi-violent encounter in the office in which van der Hoef became belligerent with a secretary, and Dr. Norcroft physically removed him from the office which created considerable animosity between her and Mr. van der Hoef and many acrimonious exchanges with his attorney, Mr. Bel Geddes.

"The most damning thing about all of that was the demonstration of fairly considerable martial arts expertise by the defendant. She was more than a match for the patient, and was more of an athlete and a self-defense expert than the rather out-of-shape and non-physical Mr. Bel Geddes. It was clear to the office girls that she would be able to overpower the man, and it became a standing office joke that she should just forget the law and meet him in a dark alley some lonely night and settle the ongoing disputes once and for all."

Burger grew wings when he heard the shotgun go off somewhere ahead of him in the trailer park's back alley clutter. Grizzly had a handgun, and van der Hoef had a shotgun. That realization was chilling. He did a remarkable job of broken field running, high jumping, dodging, and climbing until he finally got to the outer edge of the trailer park where Grizzly was standing. Burger ran up and saw—lying prone in a pile of trash—a soccer mom. There was a massive hole in her back, and it was evident that almost her entire blood volume was pooled on and around her.

"Where is he?" was his first question.

"Off in the trees in that orchard. I stopped and tried to help this poor girl. Her two children saw the whole thing, and they are completely freaked. I couldn't leave them, boss."

"Did you call it in?"

"Yeah. The cavalry and a bus is on the way. CPS is coming, too. Apparently, the children don't have any relatives anywhere nearby. I made the obvious decision that none of the bottom feeders in the trailer park would be suitable care-takers. Child Protective Services agreed."

"Okay, you hold down the fort. I'll give it a go in the fruit trees and see if I can get lucky."

"Go careful, man. This one is probably our killer of Bel Geddes, but he is certainly the killer of innocent Carol Wright. That's her name."

Grizzly began to cry softly.

In an uncharacteristically sensitive gesture, Burger put his arms around her. She cried for a few moments then shooed him away.

"Get him, partner. Dead or alive. And you be careful. Please don't get hurt."

It was a forlorn plea from the tough detective's heart.

"I'll be real wary, Grizzly. We are going to get through this; and I guarantee you that in the end, it will not go well for that miserable..." He decided not to finish his sentence because he was within earshot of the two dis-traught children.

The sirens of the advancing Antelope Valley and China Lake constabulary were now just audible in the distance. Burger loped away. This was going to be his collar, and he had blinders on. Nothing else mattered now but getting the killer before he could hurt anyone else, especially a cop. He had been to too many cop funerals and was determined never to have to go to another one.

He came into the orchard from the west. It was quiet among the neat rows of peach trees in the well cared for orchard. He moved with great caution, but as fast as he could. He was getting very tired because very frequently he had to duck-walk to be able to see under the foliage of the trees. There was nothing after he had been up and down three rows. He estimated that there were upwards of 75 or a 100 more to go. He was unsure what lay on the other sides of the orchard.

His cell phone vibrated.

"What?" he said in a hoarse breathless whisper.

"I got a call from the two PIs—Knox and Littlefeather—they work for that doctor…Norcroft, I think. Anyway, they checked in; and I told them what's going on. Turns out they know the area pretty well from another case."

"I remember them. They're okay for private cop wanna-bees," Burger said.

"They gave me some useful stuff. That orchard you're in is bordered by a big canal full of water on the north, and a major trash dump on the south. On the east is the freeway. There is a huge serious fence between the open patch and the highway. He won't be able to get through. He probably knows all that and will be heading south."

"I don't have anything better. I hear the noise in the trailer camp from all the cops. Send a big bunch up; so, they can come down from the south towards me as I come from the north. We want to contain the perp in the orchard until we can flush him out into the open. And—just as an aside—tell the commanders not to let their troops shoot me."

Burger began a zigzag traverse of the orchard pausing at random intervals to check up and down rows and to prevent van der Hoef from perceiving a pattern in his movements. It was still quiet—too quiet, as the movie Indians used to say. He was more than half way through when he began to hear the noise from the police forces advancing down from the trash pile. He stopped again and listened. He concentrated to try and differentiate the distant background noise from the many cops from any other, nearer, sounds that could be coming from the perp. With all of the men and dogs coming from the south, he knew that van der Hoef had to be getting frightened. Burger hoped he would get spooked enough to become careless, trading stealth for speed.

He moved to his right. There was a noise—some branches cracking. He waited. Another crackling noise came, and now he could tell it was coming from his left, but more or less straight in head of him. He dropped down to a squat and peered under and between the tree trunks. There was a man walking briskly at an angle towards his general direction, generally headed north towards the canal. He moved quietly but picking up speed hoping to intersect with the man. The perp was now trotting and creating steady noise that made it easy to know where he was. There were too many trees to get off a good shot, and he knew that if he yelled, van der Hoef would just spook, change direction and melt back into the center of the orchard.

The police dogs were now barking furiously. They had caught van der Hoef's scent and were straining at their leashes. Their handlers were yelling. Captains and sergeants were calling for their troops to swing towards the north. Burger saw van der Hoef take off at a sprint dodging trees. Two snarling dogs were coming at him running as fast as their legs could carry them.

Burger and van der Hoef broke cover and ran into the cleared area along the canal which was about 20 feet wide. They were 25 or 30 yards apart. They saw each other at the same time. Van der Hoef dropped down and fired a 12 gauge round in the general direction of Burger who dropped flat on the ground. The police dogs ran out of the peach tree grove as van der Hoef came within five feet of the edge of the canal. He whirled about and fired off a round which caught the lead dog in the face, and it went down without a sound.

The second dog paused for a moment by its fallen fellow officer then gave a bone cracking roar and flung itself at the kneeling criminal. Van der Hoef fired again, hitting the dog in its right shoulder and front leg. It struggled on gamely on three legs, but could not reach van der Hoef before he leaped into the canal.

Burger was sprinting as fast as his legs and lungs would allow. He saw van der Hoef start swimming across the briskly flowing canal. He had obviously jettisoned his shot gun in favor of a strong two arm stroke. He was a poor swimmer, however; and Burger was able to leap 10 feet into the water and to begin a steady hard Australian crawl on a line designed to cross van der Hoef about five feet from the opposite bank. Unfortunately for them both, the walls of the canal were concrete and stood more than six feet above the water line. The water was almost eight feet deep; so, neither man could gain a purchase by planting his feet on the bottom.

Burger pounded his strong swimming arms right over the top of van der Hoef driving him under the water. The smaller man was nearly exhausted from his flight from the trailer park and from running around in the orchard. He was not at all used to swimming and had taken in some gulps of water as he tried to fill his oxygen starved lungs. Burger's crash into him was the last straw, and he flailed under the water and began to drown. Robbery Homicide Detective Lincoln Carter dived in and swam up to Burger and van der Hoef in a few powerful strokes. Burger was fighting to hold the criminal's head out of the water, but it was a struggle.

Carter took over. He put van der Hoef in a cross chest carry and began a cautious float and swim progress downstream. All of the fight had gone out of van der Hoef. He begged Carter to save him, whimpering and choking. Burger came up alongside and helped keep van der Hoef's head out of the water. Finally, Carter was able to get a grip on a pipe that was running down the wall of the canal and to hold on long enough for Burger to help hold van der Hoef in place. Two more cops swam across, found a safety ladder and climbed out on the opposite bank.

They extended their hands to van der Hoef and pulled him out and put him in cuffs. Carter gave Burger a mighty last push which enabled him to rise high enough for the other two police officers to catch his wrists and pull him out. The effort threw Carter back into the current. He was not alarmed. He simply turned over on his back and floated comfortably downstream until he came to the next pipe and used it to get out of the water and up on the bank where he took a few nice dry gulps of clean air.

Burger turned to the other policemen and said, "You know what this guy did back in the trailer park?"

They nodded.

"Well, he also killed the lawyer, Bel Geddes. We have got to get him back to Parker Center and get a signed confession from him that we can take to the court tomorrow. Otherwise there could be a serious miscarriage of justice. Let's get him outta here as fast as we can."

As if he had uttered a prayer and divine providence was listening, a police helicopter wafted down and landed half a dozen feet from them.

"I can only take three of you," the pilot said.

"You, me, and the perp, Carter. You other two guys did great work. Sorry, you get to take a pretty good hike. We have to make good time for the rest of the day and night," Burger ordered.

Burger was impressed at how much Gerrit looked like his brother. Both men had lean, hungry, Slavic faces which belied their Dutch origins. Both were wiry and tattooed. In less than an hour the two police officers and Gerrit were sitting in the RHD interview room at Parker Center. They all had steaming mugs of coffee. Burger began with softballs and was now getting closer to the serious questions. It was nine-ten in the evening, and the center was quiet.

Chapter Ten

The trial resumed at nine a.m. on the dot. Judge Drammon was a stickler for punctuality, and he never failed to bring it up just before adjournments so that resumption of court business would be efficient. He was known to cite attorneys for contempt who made it a habit to arrive late or unprepared.

Prentiss hammered home once more on Sybil's motive and spent the next hour carefully explaining what he described as "the indisputable evidence" that Sybil had both means and opportunity. Since no gun had ever been linked to Sybil or her husband and there was no evidence of any appointment with Bel Geddes or witnesses who could place Sybil at or near the Bel Geddes residence, he knew he was on shaky ground. More than once, Sybil rolled her eyes at her attorney, taking care not to be too obvious. Prentiss asserted several times that Charles Daniels, Sybil's husband, was lying when he told the jury that she had been with him the entire time period in which the murder could have occurred.

Finally, Prentiss paused then said dramatically, "Sybil Norcroft killed Paul Bel Geddes. This shoe fits; so, you can't acquit."

There was a small murmur of laughter at his mirror image reference to the famous quote from the O.J. Simpson trial. The judge raised his gavel, and the courtroom returned to an embarrassed silence.

"She is guilty of premeditated murder. You know you feel it in your guts. You have the evidence. She is a well-known doctor, but no one is above the law. Find her guilty and let justice be done."

He sat down, satisfied that he had done the best he could. It was ten after ten.

Judge Drammon announced that he and the attorneys would meet for the next couple of hours to go over the judge's instructions to the jury.

"Take a long lunch. Think about the evidence; don't talk to each other or anyone else; rest and come back to your seats ready to hear the summation by Mr. Henley, the attorney for the defense."

The questioning of Gerrit van der Hoef went ahead with dispatch because he was very tired, very much in need of a chemical fix; and he assumed that all was lost. His life was in the crapper anyway; so, why fight it? His only hold out was due to his terrible fear of the death penalty. His life had been miserable, and he was willing to settle for more of the same in prison.

"Look, Gerrit," Burger was saying, "you and I both know we have you dead to rights. You murdered that little woman in front of her two kids and several adult witnesses. Since that was done during flight to avoid being arrested by duly sworn officers of the law—a felony—we have you for the death penalty. You have to be the most hated man in LA right now. Our difficulty will be in getting an unbiased jury."

"Any kind of a deal for me?" van der Hoef asked head down in a submissive posture.

"What're you thinking, Gerrit?"

"Maybe if I cop to the Bel Geddes thing and save everybody some grief and sweat, you could put in a word for me with the judge."

"Maybe, but it would have to be good. We're going to take down your brother, Henk, and his floozy girlfriend and Axelrod, the pawnbroker over in Nevada. That's a pretty good day for us, Gerrit, but the thought of doing less paperwork is enticing. Maybe you can give us some mitigating circumstances, and we can think about going easy on Henk."

"I ain't done much good in my life. Keepin' Henk out of the slammer might make up for some of my sins. Can I tell you my story? You can see if it will tip the scales in my direction."

"We're listening."

It is more than an old adage that 'confession is good for the soul'; it is often a real source of peace for tormented criminal consciences. Catharsis was exactly what Gerrit needed that night.

"I was a decent guy onct. I had a trade—ship building—and a good job with good pay and took care of my wife. My grandpa worked in the Westminister County boat yards making tug boats. My father had worked in the boat yards on sailing ketches, and they got me the job at the boat yards workin' on a navy contract to build variations of PT boats. I worked there for 17 years—never took a single sick day. But, near as I can recall, I had hated every second of every day I slaved away there. It was monotonous and back breaking.

Every day, I had to bend to rivet and glue, did lots of twisting and stretching to reach a corner or up inside a built-in boat locker. I finally lost my first wife because of the boat yard; the place made me so jumpy and mad all the time that she had finally left me—ran away with a shoe salesman. I don't blame her or the shoe man, just the boat yard.

"My back got to hurtin' all of the time, lasted for years. I guess I can't really remember for sure when I didn't have no back pain. I guess that I didn't like the pain any more than any other sane man, but I sort of reached a steady state—that's what the company doctor said—with my discomfort. It was always there. It was kind of like my second wife who was never satisfied with anything I ever did, didn't like that I took a drink with guys from work. She never shut up. Anyway, I think that the worst thing about it was that I still had to work.

"I seen the company doctors a dozen times or more for my back pain. They just told me to 'suck it up' or to 'get more exercise'; some of the time they put me on bed rest for a couple of days or made me go through a couple of weeks of physical therapy. At least, that got me off work for a couple of hours three times a week for those two weeks if the doctor was young or new on the job.

"I kept askin' them about getting' permanent disability. They gave me the same answer every time, 'No, you are not eligible for permanent medical disability for this little back pain.' Little to them, but big for me. Worse, none of them would give me a prescription for oxycontin. I knew it was the only thing that would work.

"I went and seen a orthopedic surgeon onct. He hardly looked at me and never put a hand on me. I brought up the idea of permanent disability, and he said somethin' snotty, like 'if you want to get off work permanently, you'll have to stick a pin in your eye, or accidentally on purpose, cut off a thumb. I knew I was bein' dissed, but you can't fight the know-it-all docs or the company bosses. So, I just had to put up with it. I was miserable. I hated the work, and I got started on booze and some oxycontin Henk got me from somebody who worked in a pharmacy and could steal a little now and then.

"What happened to get me involved with that 'Snow Queen' neurosurgeon and eventually that miserable excuse for a human bein', Bel Geddes, was that, one day on the job I lifted a box of rivets and twisted to set the box inside the hull of the punt I was workin' on. The box wasn't even all that heavy. But the pain started to change—to get real bad. What made me get worried was that this time, I also developed pain that started in my right butt and shot all the way down my leg to the toes, and it was far worse than any of my back pain had ever been.

"Finally, the foreman took me off shift and demanded that I go to see the quacks at the company clinic. By then, my back was swolled up and stiff from the pain, and my right leg hurt like the worst toothache in my life. The doc was rough with me. He raised my right leg straight off the gurney. I got terrible pain and tingling all the way down my poor leg, and I yelled. He gave me a shot of Demerol which helped for a day, but the pain got worse, not better after that. If I moved or strained or coughed or just about anything, it was awful. I went back to the company quack and begged like a little kid for him to do somethin', anythin'—cut my leg off, whatever. By then it hurt to pee, to take a dump; and my sex life disappeared. That is a lot of the reason my first wife left me. The shoe salesman seemed like a better catch. They gave me a few more shots. I smoked like a fiend and somebody got me started on meth. I was a complete mess.

"At long, long last, the company quack sent me off to see the specialist surgeon. She was that Norcroft dame who's on trial for killing that creep, Bel Geddes. I keep up with the news, ya know.

"I told her 'I can't stand it, Doc. You gotta do somethin'. I'm dyin'. I gotta have surgery, or somebody's gotta shoot me. Somethin'. I gotta have a CT or some sorta test. I'm never gonna be able to work again. What am I gonna do?'

"The stingy company and its insurance made me wait even though Dr. Norcroft said I needed an MRI. Finally, after what seemed like forever, I got a foot drop; all of a sudden it became an emergency. Lickedigosplit I got admitted to the hospital, had an MRI, and was operated on, like this was the first time I ever told anybody about my troubles."

"How'd you do with the operation?" Carter interjected a question.

"Man, it was great. I got almost all better. Still had the same old smoulderin' back pain, but I had gotten used to that. Norcroft refused to give me a permanent disability chit, and I finally was forced to go back to the yards again. The pain all came back again. I guess I had it wrong. But, I eventually learned that the pain was in the opposite side and at a different level. I seen Bel Geddes because I needed money, and his ads said that he could deliver. He convinced me to lie and say that it was the same thing as before. When it was proved different, he made me lie and say that she had operated on the wrong side. I still couldn't get permanent disability. Oh, I forgot; the Snow Queen operated on me again—on the other side."

Carter shook his head, "And how did that go, Gerrit?"

"Just okay. I got better, but not all better. I was drinkin', smokin', and takin' pain pills like M&Ms; and by then I was hooked on meth and oxy. I don't think I could tell by then what was real and what was not. They forced me to go into a work hardening program. The PT guy in charge called me a malingerer."

"Bel Geddes started a suit against Dr. Norcroft, the boat yard, and the insurance company. Bel Geddes was lazy, and I think he was afraid of the nasty ice-berg of a doctor. He kept stringin' me along with promises of depositions and gettin' into court; so, I could have my day. Nothin' ever happened. I finally learned that he ducked out of depositions; he couldn't find an expert witness against Dr. Norcroft—I think it was because he never tried at all—and finally, after eleven years, he just shut down the case without so much as a 'by-the-way' to me. I ended up a bum without a job, no wife, no friends except maybe my brother, Henk; and I was addicted. I had to steal to live. I knocked over more little convenience stores than I can remember. I did a couple of stretches in the High Desert Prison in Lancaster and a nickel in San Quentin. During that time, all I had to think about was how to get money and how to get back at Bel Geddes. I kind of got less hateful towards Dr. Norcroft, like maybe she didn't really do nothin' wrong. Still, she treated me bad; and I wouldn't have cared if she got run over by a bus.

"Henk knew the house cleaner that worked for Bel Geddes and his fancy-schmancy little trophy wife. She told him— and he told me—about the safe with all its money and diamonds in it and like how the big brilliant lawyer couldn't remember to close the thing up most of the time. Henk got Maria—that was the maid's name—to slip him a key to the front gate and the house. She also told him the door password. He had to get some of his friends to arrange a safe boat trip from Ensenada to LA for her whole family. Maria knew that the coyotes who took the wet backs and the dry feets across the desert would as soon kill them as look at them. She was very grateful. I mean, veeery grateful, if you get my meanin'. Henk and Maria took up with each other.

"Maria let us know when Bel Geddes and his wife were out for the evening. So, Henk drove me to their place. I lost my license after a few DUIs. Anyway, he went and hid a few blocks away. I had my 12 gauge riot gun hid under a black trench coat so's no looky-loos would see it. I played ninja and broke in. That was a piece of cake. But, my luck turned rotten as usual. Seems big lawyer, Bel Geddes, didn't go out after all. I was makin' a beeline for the open safe when who should walk into the hallway but the man himself. He recognized me right off. I wasn't wearin' my ski mask like I should of; it was itchy. He yelled at me. I pulled out my 12 gauge. He ran towards the safe to close it up. I just pumped in a round and blasted him without even thinkin' what I was doin'. It liked ta blown the back of his head off. I all but peed my pants.

"But, I was sure that the blast from the shotgun would bring the neighbors and the cops. It was as loud as a cannon, I thought. I had a gym bag with me, and I run over and shoveled a huge pile of cash and about twenty or thirty pounds of jewelry into it. They looked fake because they were so big. I ran outta there like a scalded cat. Henk was waitin' out front. He had heard the shot and rushed back. We got clean away."

"Who took care of the loot?" Burger asked.

"Me and Henk divided it up 50-50. He knew a pawn broker who was a good fence who never opened his mouth about where stuff come from. Henk drove up to Pawrump and found his old flame, a part-time ho name of Fancy— probably a fake name, I guess—who he gave a few bucks to deliver the goods. We got about 300 K outta that. I know it was worth maybe eight mil, but a doper like me is happy to get enough for his next fix. I kept about half of mine—hid it in my home-crap-home, as a movie actor once called his place. That was a big mistake."

"And that's why you took off when my woman partner and I came out to your trailer house in China Lake. You were afraid that we'd find the rest of the loot, and you would be caught and bring down Henk with you," said Burger.

"That's about the size of it," Gerrit said. "I ran. I ran like I was in good shape. Like to of killed me."

"Why'd you shoot the young mother and right in front of her two kids, Gerrit? Why'd you do that?" Burger asked, gritting his teeth.

"Man, I was so pumped. I wasn't gonna let anythin' or anybody get in my way. The lady detective was right on my tail. I had the shotgun in my hand. It's almost like it had a mind of its own. It just went off and blasted that woman. I was on meth at the moment; and when a dude is on meth, he don't care about nobody else. I just run off into the orchard then, and left the detective lady to try and save the woman. I knew the orchard real well and figgered I could get through it and outta there before any other cops could come in there to get me. I hadn't counted on you leavin' your partner with the dead woman and roarin' after me. I guess that's about it. You know the rest of the history, and here we are."

"Yeah, here we are," said Burger.

"So, you'll keep me from gettin' the needle and let Henk off the hook? I owe him that much, and you owe me for what I give you. Save you a ton a work."

"I'll ring the DA on call and see what I can do. I'll give it my best. Now, Gerrit, you got one more thing to do. It's a lot of work. But I need you to write everything down you just told me. Here's some yellow legal paper and a dozen pens. We have a recording of everything you said. Detective Carter will help you get it done, but you have to do all of the writing; and you have to sign a paper saying we did not force you, okay."

"Okay."

"So, Gerrit, let me ask you one more question. Do you feel better now that it is all out, that you made a full confession."

Gerrit looked more relaxed and was giving in to his exhaustion.

"Ya know, I really do."

Chapter Eleven

While Gerrit van der Hoek and his detectives slept away their exhaustion then refueled to get the report finalized, Judge Drammon's court began to come alive. The court reporter, security personnel, and janitors arrived at about the same time and got their preparations done so when the judge arrived, everything would be ready. The judge had admonished all of the attorneys that this case had to get to the jury in time for them to begin preliminary discussions.

At nine o-clock on the dot, the courtroom stood in respect for the entrance of his honor; and Jack Henley began to deliver his summation to the jury on behalf of his client, Sybil Norcroft.

"Ladies and gentlemen of the jury. You have been patient, worked hard, and paid attention during what has been a fairly long trial. The pay is low for your work, but what you are doing is very important to our civil society. The issues here are crucial. A man is dead—quite obviously murdered. Someone, sometime, must pay for that. A woman of great importance to our city is on trial here with her reputation, her livelihood, her freedom, and perhaps even her life, at risk. Your job is difficult. The evidence is confusing, and I will make every effort to make it more simple to understand. As you were instructed by the judge, your decision must be what the legal term says, 'beyond a reasonable doubt'. That is more than a preponderance of evidence, the lesser requirement used in civil cases. But it is not so great as to be beyond *all* doubt.

"This is the question: did Sybil Norcroft, with malice aforethought, kill another human being, Paul Devon Bel Geddes? Consider the three issues: did she have motive enough to convince you that Dr. Norcroft would deem it in her best interest to murder a man who has admittedly tormented her for over a decade. What would she gain? Money? I don't think so. She is wealthy. Did she do it anyway because of some distorted greed? There has not been a single shred of evidence that any of Mr. Bel Geddes's belongings, including cash, ever came into the possession of Dr. Norcroft. I will not belabor that. It has been the prosecution's burden of proof, and they have failed to identify evidence for such a motive. Could the motive be simply to remove a thorn in her shoe, so's to speak. Mr. Bel Geddes was intentionally disrespectful and overtly dedicated to persecuting my client, Sybil Norcroft. Did she kill him to get him out of her hair? She has had over a decade to do so, why now? Really, do you think this highly educated and accomplished woman would consider such a recourse? Let me put it simply. The answer is no; and again, the prosecution has failed to offer evidence that Dr. Norcroft did, in fact, murder Mr. Bel Geddes or any evidence that her character is such that it is beyond a reasonable doubt to attribute such violent qualities to her.

"So, let us consider the means. Is there any evidence—*any evidence whatever*—that Sybil Norcroft or her husband or her associates owned a shotgun or any other gun, for that matter? None! The prosecution failed in its duty to produce evidence that Dr. Norcroft had the means. Did she have the opportunity? She could not have been in two places at once. She has an alibi. Incidentally, the word comes from the Latin for "in another place, elsewhere." The time of the murder has been well identified by the Los Angeles medical examiner. It occurred between ten and midnight. That is an uncontested fact. Charles Daniels—a man of unimpeachable character—testified in this court that Dr. Norcroft was with him essentially every minute during and after that period of time. He described their activities delicately, "We went to bed at nine, got better acquainted, watched TV until ten..." That is pretty descriptive and has the ring of truth. The district attorney made innuendoes that Mr. Daniels lied; he produced no evidence. The district attorney made innuendoes that Dr. Norcroft could have sneaked into the well secured mansion owned by the Bel Beddeses. Again, no proof. None. My esteemed opponent further suggested the possibility that Dr. Norcroft hired or persuaded an unknown subject to kill Mr. Bel Geddes. Was there any evidence, anything, to verify that? There's a pattern here, and this is getting monotonous, isn't it? There is none.

"Ladies and gentlemen of the jury. I will not take up more of your time. You have heard the facts such as they are. I serve only to point out the salient facts there was no real motive, no means, and no opportunity. Logic demands an acquittal. Your good common sense must also believe beyond a reasonable doubt that Sybil Norcroft is innocent, not just not guilty because of insufficient evidence. Please do your duty and set this fine woman free. Then the police can do their duty and find the real killer. Thank you."

Everyone in the courtroom was mildly astonished at the brevity of the defense's summation. It was only ten-forty in the morning.

"The jury will receive my instructions and then adjourn to the jury room to begin its deliberations. You are first to understand that in matters of the law, you are bound by my instructions. Any error will be my responsibility. You must base your verdict on information in full conformance with the following instructions…:"

His instructions occupied over half an hour. The jury was excused, and the attorneys returned to their separate offices. To their great surprise, they were summoned back to the court only fifteen minutes later. Both sides fretted and sweated that such a short period of deliberation did not bode well for their side.

When everyone was seated, Judge Drammon addressed the jury, "Madam Foreperson, have you reached a verdict?"

There was an awkward pause. The foreperson looked up and met the judge's serious gaze, "No, your honor, we are deadlocked."

There was an audible murmur in the courtroom which was shushed with one rap of Judge Drammon's gavel.

"That is unacceptable, Madam Foreperson and members of the jury. You are ordered to return and put in the necessary work as finders of the facts to reach a unanimous verdict. You have not put in enough hard work yet," he chided. "Get back in there and make more cogent arguments, test the evidence, find the inconsistencies. Come back when you have a verdict. You are excused."

Everyone went to his or her own place to begin the waiting again.

Sybil said to Jack Henley, "I feel like I am being twisted on an unwinding rope. I don't know how much more of this I can take."

"Apparently, we haven't truly begun the difficult part," Henley said, "hang in there."

Gerrit's handwriting was surprisingly legible. He wrote in entirely large cap letters, and they were plain. It was odd, but, in a way, more convincing. Burger was glad that the writing, paragraph and sentence structure, and syntax were evidence of a fairly sound mind—one that could not be challenged as being impaired. This morning he was clear-headed, having slept off most of the chemically induced deficiencies in his performance the previous evening. The detectives had had van der Hoef hold off before affixing his signature to his work. They wanted a video of him doing so in order to prevent any suggestion that he had been coerced.

It was eight in the morning. Burger knew that in an hour the trial where the neurosurgeon, Dr. Norcroft, was fighting for her life was going to start what might well be its last day. He also knew that the yellow legal sheets he held in his hands were the key to her acquittal, exoneration, and freedom. It was a satisfying feeling for a cop to be able to make a serious difference in how things turned out. He went into the holding cells area and roused van der Hoef.

"Okay, Gerrit, time to rise and shine. You did good work last night. We need to get up and get going. I got Henk to bring you in a suit to wear for the video we talked about. All we have left is to have your signature on these sheets, and our deal goes into effect. Here's the agreement about your plea and the recommended sentence and Henk's guarantee of immunity."

Gerrit blinked his eyes and slowly came around. He swung his legs over the edge of the cot and rubbed them vigorously to restore life in them. His eyes cleared, and he took a long look at Burger.

"I ain't gonna sign them papers," he said.

"What did you just say?!"

"You heard me. I decided to fight this thing. I been a fighter alla my life, and this is just another fight. I'm not gonna let myself git railroaded like that neurosurgeon doc and that crooked lawyer done to me that ruined my life. Nosiree, I am gonna fight this."

He had not said the nuclear-blast word, "attorney" yet. Burger was reeling, but there was still some time. He had to be very careful about this.

"Look, Gerrit, you're real tired after your long night. I'll get you a good breakfast, then we'll talk again."

"Okay, but I'm not budgin'."

Burger felt desperate. He could see the scenario unfolding as if he were watching a movie: Gerrit holds fast to his stubborn refusal; Norcroft gets convicted; Len Prentiss, the preening Hollywood climber of a DA, digs in his heels and refuses to accept that he could have been wrong and won't work with LAPD to overturn the conviction; Gerrit goes down for the murder of the mom in the trailer park, but he can't be tried for the Bel Geddes murder because the majesty of the law has already spoken. Courts are notoriously reluctant to overturn the work of prosecutors and juries. At best it would be several years before the creaky wheels of justice turned around to free Norcroft—years from now. Her life would be wrecked, and she was innocent. What a mess.

At noon, Sybil was returned to her cell at the county jail to await the return of the jury. Her husband, Charles Daniels, her attorneys, Jack Henley and Rupert Ortega, private eyes, Drew Knox and Amber Littlefeather, closeted together in the jail interview room waiting on pins and needles for the jury to return.

Drew took center stage, "I talked to Anson Burger, the LAPD lead detective a couple of times last night. Everything was a go with the real killer's—Gerrit van der Hoef—confession. This morning at seven-thirty, Burger had the completed document in hand. But…"

Everyone groaned. There was that hated word, "but."

"But, Burger called me about five minutes ago to tell me that for some unknown reason, the creep now refuses to sign. He doesn't actually recant the confession, but he just wants to take his chances in court. Ultimately, he will be convicted of the young woman in the trailer court's murder; but if Dr. Norcroft is convicted of the murder of Paul Bel Geddes, even if it is a mistake, it will take forever—like as long as five years, maybe more—to get Dr. Norcroft out of prison. And—even with overwhelming evidence to the contrary—the system may balk and refuse to grant a re-trial in the end. I'm sorry, I can't see what more there is to do."

"We know van der Hoef did it. We have evidence to seal a verdict in an open-and-shut case, and yet I am still in terrible jeopardy. That about it?" Sybil said.

All color had drained from her face. She seemed to have shrunk.

"At the moment, but we are going to be on the line with Burger and his partner, the one they call Grizzly. They are very resourceful and tough minded. We have hope, Sybil. I think they can still pull a rabbit out of the hat," Jack said.

Charles put his arm around Sybil. He cried. She didn't. She just stared into space. There were demons in that space.

At eleven-ten, a request came from the jury room for copies of the GSR residue. It was provided. Half an hour later a request came for a transcript of the testimony of all witnesses who had heard Dr. Norcroft threaten Mr. Bel Geddes. Nerves were frayed all around: the judge, all of the attorneys, the jurors, and, not incidentally, those of the defendant and her husband. At Parker Center, Burger and Grizzly thought their nerves would crack; or they would strangle the stubborn idiot, Gerrit van der Hoef.

Burger made three more appeals to van der Hoef. The only success was that the perp had still not outright asked for an attorney, but Burger knew it was only a matter of time.

"I have an idea," he said. "Let's go talk to Henk."

Henk van der Hoef had brought clothes for Gerrit in case he had to make an appearance in court that day. He had been cooling his heels in the waiting room watching cartoons since he turned the clothes over to Grizzly earlier in the morning. He was bored out of his mind, and he was growing steadily more impatient.

Burger and Grizzly strode into the waiting room.

"About time," Henk said. "Can I get outta here now?"

"We have a problem with Gerrit, Henk. One that involves you," Burger said.

That got Henk's full attention.

"How me?"

"This morning we had a full confession for the murders in hand and a deal to let you off scot free and for Gerrit to avoid the death penalty. That deal was signed and notarized by the mayor, the police commissioner, and the attorney general."

"So what kinda problem could there be?" Henk asked, looking worried.

"You know Gerrit better than we do. He won't sign. He is ready to get a rookie public defender assigned by the court and to get his say said in court even though he risks the death penalty. I have to tell you, Henk, that is almost a sure thing."

"What about me?" Henk asked, with the light bulb over his head beginning to light up.

"I think you know. You go all the way with him as an accomplice. I suppose you could get the needle as well. The best you could hope for is life without parole. Think you could talk sense into your brother?"

"He owes me for a lifetime of big favors. I'll give it my best shot."

"Let's get in there. We only have a very short time before it is too late to save the doctor from a verdict of guilty by the jury. If that happens, Henk, you know all deals are off. We won't need you anymore. Because that's a real possibility, I'm going to put you in handcuffs now before we go see your brother."

"Is that really necessary, Detective? I mean, I'm here almost in the lock-up."

"It might convince Gerrit that we mean business. If nothing else, it is kind of good theater."

"Okay, let's get on with it."

The jury sent out a request for the answer to a question. "How long before GSR clears from the skin and clothes even after washings?" Judge Drammon directed the court reporter to copy the relevant police expert's testimony and sent it into the jury room.

All interested parties were kept abreast of developments. Sybil asked Jack what he thought it meant.

"Sorry, Doc. I long ago gave up trying to read the minds of juries. I can't see how the questions would suggest them leaning for or against you. We will just have to wait."

The jail interview room settled into glum silence again. Sybil and Charles sat holding each other in an anguished embrace. It was as if they were waiting for a beloved relative to die.

Grizzly asked Burger if he thought it was safe for Henk to be alone with Gerrit. Who knows what Henk might do if Gerrit chose to drag his brother down with him in the end? Burger insisted on her being in the room with the two brothers. Both detectives thought that maybe the presence of a woman would be a more relaxing touch than having the tough-looking old veteran detective running the show.

Burger could see and hear what was going on. The men in front of the one-way window chatted for a few minutes about old times. Henk talked about what a brute their alcoholic father had been and how their mother had never stuck up for them. Gerrit just nodded in agreement. After about five minutes, Henk began to speak to his brother in earnest.

"Gerrit, I saved your skinny little tail lots of times from Pa. Look at my arms."

Gerrit looked away. He did not want to be reminded. Henk rolled up his sleeves and showed Gerrit four perfectly round scars on each forearm.

"Remember what these came from?"

"Yeah."

"Tell me."

"Pa put out his cigarette on you."

Gerrit looked like he might cry.

"Why'd he do that?"

"Cause he thought you stole the money out of his wallet—his drinkin' money."

"Who did steal it, Gerrit?"

"I did it. Jeez, Henk, I was scared to death. I was just little, couldn't have been more than six years old."

Now, he did begin to shed tears. The memory was overwhelming.

"So, why didn't he burn you? And how come I got the whip scars on my back for when you broke his guitar?"

"I know, I know. You took the blame. You saved me. He made me look while he put out the cig on your skin. I could smell your skin burn. I bawled like a baby, and he cuffed me. He said, 'let that be a lesson to you, boy.'"

"You do remember about how you came to me for help with the Bel Geddes thing, how I got you outta there, how I took care of the money and jewelry for you, and how I never cheated you outta nothin', don't you brother?"

He put his arm around Gerrit's shoulders.

"Gerrit, I want to live. I don't want to go to the big house and die in prison. There's nothin' you can do for yourself except maybe avoid the death penalty. I'm your brother. It's your turn to take the burnin'. Save me, Gerrit. Please, I'm beggin' you."

Gerrit broke down and cried unabashedly.

"I'll do it," he said softly.

Burger and Grizzly rushed the paper to Gerrit's side, turned on the video and recorded him signing the confession documents—every page.

"We are all going to the court, right now," Burger said. "Lights and sirens. Grizzly, call ahead. I want a clear path. If you pray, say one now that we can get there on time."

The jury informed the bailiff that they had reached a verdict. He informed the judge, all the lawyers; and because he had been slipped a Benjamin by the *Times* reporter, Doug Howard, he gave him a heads-up as well.

The Sybil Norcroft party was escorted out of the jail by guards. Sybil was in wrist and ankle restraints and dressed in her best Armani suit. She had to travel by police van. The rest rushed to their cars.

Judge Drammon waited impatiently for everyone to gather before calling in the jury.

"Everyone here and accounted for?" he asked.

Although it was not really necessary, he went through the formality of having an audible roll-call. The reporters—all with their secret court building informants—began to gather like buzzards smelling a carcass.

"All right, Bailiff, summon the jury," the judge ordered.

Within a block from the old Parker Center, just off Los Angeles Street going onto San Pedro, there was a traffic snarl. They could still see "The Glass House" as the Center was widely known. Burger and Grizzly cursed and fumed. Grizzly got out and found a traffic cop and explained their problem, and a miracle occurred. The sidewalks along San Pedro were cleared, and the police vehicle rushed through. They roared through yellow and red lights and although there were no accidents, there were a couple of dozen miracles before they pulled to a stop and parked illegally in front of the Clara Shortridge Foltz Criminal Justice Center on West Temple.

Burger told Grizzly to bring both brothers, with Gerrit still in chains. He bounded up the front steps and raced along the first floor hallway towards Judge Drammon's court—room 7.

"Has the jury reached a verdict in the matter of California versus Norcroft, docket number 2013-07-XV777490?" Judge Drammon asked.

"We have, your honor," the foreperson said.

It was two-twenty-one in the afternoon. The tension in the courtroom could not have been higher.

Well, maybe that was wrong. Before the bailiff could retrieve the folded verdict sheet, the front door burst in and a disheveled man in a grey suit burst in.

"What is the meaning of this intrusion?" Judge Drammon shouted. "Guards, stop that man."

Burger was out of breath, but he managed to get out, "Judge, hold the proceedings. Please!"

"What?" the judge demanded.

Burger evaded the guards who now had their guns out.

"Judge, please hear me out. I am Detective Lieutenant Anson Burger, LAPD RHD." He held up his cred-pack. "I have hard evidence that is crucial to your proceedings and the verdict."

He huffed out a couple of more breaths trying to regain his capacity to both breathe and to speak.

"Your honor, this is highly irregular. Maybe criminal," protested the assistant DA.

"Let's hear what he has to say," Jack Henley said, grasping at any straw for his client.

The room quieted down. All eyes were on Burger. A quarter of a minute later, Grizzly and the two sullen van der Hoef brothers walked in. A security guard led them to seats in the rear.

"What is it, Detective?" the judge asked. "This better be good or you are going to cool your heals in the lock-up for a couple of weeks."

"I'll be brief, but please let me start from the beginning. I have a signed confession. You can read it while I talk. Most of what you need to know is contained on those yellow legal pages."

"I demand to see those papers first," shouted Prentiss.

He was standing and gesticulating.

"Sit down and be quiet," the judge ordered in his most magisterial voice.

Jack Henley, Sylvia, and all of their retinue saw the wisdom in keeping a low profile.

Lt. Burger then told the entire story of how Gerrit van der Hoef fell under suspicion, outlined the evidence against him, and about how he was captured in China Lake. He explained the circumstances of obtaining the confession—most of them, at least—and concluded with the definitive statement, "Your honor, ladies and gentlemen of the jury, Mr. Prentiss, the defendant, Sybil Norcroft, is not guilty. It is accurate to say that she is truly innocent. Please accept my information. If you need to hear from the actual murderer himself, he is here in the courtroom right now and ready to testify."

Judge Drammon was quiet for a moment.

"Lt. Burger, attorneys, my chambers now. Bailiff, return the jurors to the jury room and not a word from anyone about their present unread verdict."

In the judge's chambers, Prentiss started to speak, but Drammon shushed him.

"In a minute," he said while he perused the confession.

"I presume you can back up everything here, Lieutenant?" Drammon asked.

Burger said, "I can. We have an open-and-shut airtight case. The accused will plead guilty in return for a few considerations including immunity for his brother and for taking the death penalty off the table."

"That remains to be seen in another courtroom, Lieutenant; but for today in this courtroom, we seem to be able to come to a conclusion."

He handed the yellow sheets to DA Prentiss. The DA motioned for the defense attorneys to gather with his team; so, they could all read the confession at the same time.

"I guess that about takes care of the issues in this trial," Henley said.

He avoided anything that even smacked of a victory smirk.

Prentiss stood up.

"I was very much convinced by our case. As much as I am shocked to have to admit it, I guess I can only agree and request a dismissal of all charges," he said looking like a boy who had just lost his puppy.

"I think we all agree," the judge said, "unless the defense and Dr. Norcroft wish to enter a protest."

He smiled. They smiled. And they all marched back into the courtroom. The judge re-summoned the jurors, and DA Prentiss dropped the bombshell.

"Ladies and gentlemen of the jury, we have just received startling news related to this case. Los Angeles's finest have done their work and found a killer who has confessed, have ample evidence to corroborate his confession, and has the man in custody. Judge Drammon, the prosecution requests that all charges against the defendant, Sybil Norcroft, be dismissed."

"Granted," intoned the judge and banged his gavel.

It was over.

Chapter Twelve

For three days after the nerve wracking finis of Sybil's trial, she and Charles made themselves scarce and enjoyed a mind-numbing series of Broadway plays. They stayed in the Marriott Marquis in the heart of New York, and reveled in their obscurity. Reality intruded on Monday morning when she returned to her office to see eighty-one patients—the 'must-sees' she had neglected during her period of incarceration and trial. She was exhausted at the end of the day, and went to bed at eight o'clock. The following day she performed a frontal craniotomy for a pre-frontal meningioma—a benign tumor—a gross total removal of a huge right temporal glioblastoma multiforme—the most malignant primary brain tumor—and two large lumbar laminectomies for lumbar stenosis—which were slowly causing the loss of the patients' use of their legs. The next day—a special operating day for Sybil to try and catch-up—was no less demanding. By the end of the week, she had attended four meetings, met with an even hundred well-wishers from the hospital and community's elite and rank-and-file to hear them congratulate her on her acquittal and return to her surgical practice. It was exhausting but satisfying.

The next week had nearly the same start, but the end of the week was altogether different. Michael Strong, the administrator of Joseph Noble Memorial Hospital, requested a meeting with Sybil in his office. The request came in the form of a formal typed note on hospital letter-head paper, and seemed to Sybil to be every bit a summons.

"Thank you for coming, Dr. Norcroft," Mr. Strong said and gestured for her to take a seat in his private office.

Since he usually called her by her first name, the formality of the initial greeting made Sybil's social antennae perk up to the warning point.

"Michael," she said, and offered her hand.

After the handshake, the administrator said, "I am delighted at the verdict from your trial and the complete vindication it represents. Here at the hospital, there was never a doubt about that outcome."

"Thank you, Michael. However, I can't help thinking that there is a 'but' in there somewhere. What's up?"

Mr. Strong's hale-fellow-well-met smile faded, and his face took on an uneasy serious look.

"As difficult as this is, there is something that I must discuss with you. As you can well imagine, the notoriety of the arrest, the trial, and the speculations surrounding your actions have reflected badly on the hospital. Our donors have become leery and are withholding donations. A number of the hospital staff members have registered concerns about patient admission rates and about unwanted scrutiny on their practices from governmental and concerned citizen groups since the whole sad scenario began. Our governing board held a special Monday evening meeting regarding your status."

"My status?!" Sybil asked, unable to control the hint of alarm in her voice.

"I'm afraid so, much as it personally distresses me."

"And who, might I ask, was invited to that meeting to talk about me?"

It was the incisive direct question for which Dr. Norcroft was famous.

"I can't really say."

"Can't or won't, Michael.? Which is it?"

"Both, I guess. Listen, Dr. Norcroft, none of us can control public opinion. The board of directors has become justifiably alarmed. We have never had a scandal hit the hospital of this magnitude; it has been in the local and national news for months. Our integrity has come under attack. Frankly, the board has determined that we must cut our losses, and that we must do so publicly."

Sybil was now fully alarmed.

"So, exactly what does that mean, Mr. Strong? Do I get thrown under the bus?"

"Nothing like that, but there are consequences. I'm sure you realize that the status quo would not prevail after such a long and devastating exposure of the hospital."

"Cut to the chase, Mr. Strong. What is being proposed?"

"Again, I dislike being in this position, but the board is beyond proposing. I am afraid that the board chair, Mildred Hankin…"

"Darryl Hankin's wife…the chief of ENT's wife?"

"I'm afraid so."

"Hardly a fair and objective board meeting, I surmise. Darryl is my most public enemy on the hospital staff, has been since before the Brendan McNeely case. But I'm interrupting. Go ahead."

"The board chair, speaking for a nearly unanimous board has asked for…in fact demanded your resignation from the staff."

The verbalization of such a devastating statement was as much of a blow as if Sybil had been punched in the solar plexus by a professional fighter. She was speechless for a few minutes.

"Are you all right?" Mr. Strong asked, genuinely concerned.

"I have most certainly been better, thank you for asking."

"Because of the board's decision—which I have to assure you is final—the hospital central committee met in emergency session and has voted by a slim majority to revoke your admitting and surgical privileges. Mrs. Hankin insists that all of this be announced to the *LA Times* and local TV."

"It would be demeaning for me even to ask for a hearing on this absurd ruling. As to the public announcement, have you gone completely nuts? Apparently you have no concept of the depth of my fury, and even less of a notion of what the suit I will launch will do to your precious hospital's reputation. I am being driven out by a thoroughly sexist cabal because I am a successful woman who has been a more effective competitor than the old-boy network. I am still the president of the National Women-in-Medicine Organization and am the president-elect of the Professional Women's Feminist League—two million strong with more than 600,000 in California alone. How do you think they will react to this? Hmmh? Did you really think I would take this lying down, that I would be submissive like the rest of the far-right Republican women whose husbands practice medicine and mediaeval politics on the staff here and in the city? Get real!"

Ice water dripped from her every word. Michael Strong began to be afraid.

"Now, look, Sybil…"

"Keep it 'Dr. Norcroft', Mr. Strong. We are past the pleasantries, and we are not buddies."

"Now, now…"

"And you can skip any platitudes. I won't be buying them."

"So, how can we work this out and avoid…unpleasantness?"

"*Unpleasantness*!!?? What a dainty term. What you want to avoid, let me tell you, is a $100 million suit. I am sure you know something of my resources. You won't have a job a week after the suit is filed, and the hospital's insurance company will be glad to settle at half of that figure in a month to avoid further losses. You want to make it public?! You have no idea what public is. I have been a supporter of gay-marriage, women's choice, gay-rights, women's rights to equal pay for equal work for decades, and have contributed to the campaigns of the past two governors, three senators, and three congress people to say nothing of all my well-known help in the state legislature. The people who run those campaigns are my friends. They have media access you can only dream of. Don't even think of making me into some minor media spectacle to humor the bigots on the board and the staff, Mr. Strong. Now let's talk business."

At Sybil's request, Mr. Strong summoned the hospital's attorneys, and they 'got down to business'. When that morning's meeting was over, it was agreed that Sybil would resign from the staff quietly for reasons of upcoming career changes. Because of her contractual arrangement with the hospital to bring her patients to JNMH exclusively—which was worth more than $22 million a year—the hospital would pay her a severance of four million dollars amortized over four years. There would be…to put it nicely…a gag order imposed on the board, the officers of the medical staff, and on Sybil and her husband. Severe financial penalties were attached for failure to comply. Her departure from JNMH would take place at the end of two months while she made arrangements for the care of her large patient load; Sybil agreed not to steer her patients to other hospitals. The hospital agreed to hold a major black-tie gala to show its appreciation for the many years of service of its distinguished head of surgery. The gala was to be a fund-raiser for breast cancer and attendance by every member of the board and the medical staff officers was to be mandatory in order to retain their continuing hospital privileges.

With unprecedented alacrity, the documents were signed by the end of the following week, and Sybil Norcroft was left to contemplate life without Joseph Noble Memorial Hospital, her professional home since she finished her neurosurgery residency. She and the hospital were scrupulous about remaining silent about the arrangements of her leaving JNMH, but the fact of her impending departure itself quickly became public knowledge. Mr. Strong and Mrs. Hankin were quoted in the paper and on television lauding the remarkable accomplishments of their premier surgeon and expressing their regret at her personal choice. She was destined for bigger and better things, and the hospital's loss would be the Dr. Norcroft's next choice's gain, etc., etc. Sybil was in high demand on the LGBT, and feminism circuits and gave keynote addresses at the annual clinical congress meeting of the American College of Surgeons and the combined meeting of the American Association of Neurological Surgeons and the Congress of Neurosurgeons.

Her star was in the ascendency, and she appeared to be at the zenith of her career. She was heralded as being strong and something of a heroine for having weathered the criminal charges that were widely regarded as an attack against her for her gender and her feminist views. Her fame—which she knew would be fleeting—brought her highly prestigious appointments to the AANS Board of Directors, the regional chairmanship of the AMA, and the vice-chairmanship of the California Board of Medical Licensure. What she really needed was a job.

Her husband, Charles made the first important suggestion.

"Sybil, you don't really have to spend the rest of your life and career in California. We have a serious opportunity for a change that you might be able to capitalize on. The company's board of directors wants me to relocate our headquarters to Washington D.C.; so, we can expand our international enterprises, especially in South and Central America. You have the contacts now; how about using them to wangle yourself an appointment to one of the medical schools in the D.C. area?"

"I'll give it serious thought, Charles. I like the idea."

She did not need to 'wangle' very hard. She dropped the idea of her beginning an academic career during a meeting of the AANS Funding Committee; she was overheard by the chairman of the neurosurgery department of Georgetown University School of Medicine—a fellow member of the board of the National Women-in-Medicine Organization, of which Sybil was the president. Dr. Harriet Winslow had ambitions of becoming the president of the AANS; she would be the first woman to hold that position, and she wanted Sybil's support to get her to one more stepping stone, that of being the president of the NWMO when Sybil finished her term. Their mutual ambitions meshed well, and two months later, Sybil Norcroft, M.D., Ph.D., F.A.C.S. was an associate professor and vice-chairperson of the Department of Neurosurgery at Georgetown University.

That announcement, along with the favorable media coverage of her acquittal, and the anti-feminist undertones of the whole affair captured the attention of Wolf News. They were interested because they wanted to be able to compete with WWN's photogenic, brilliant, and extremely ·popular multiple Emmy award winning chief medical correspondent, Raja Patel, M.D. In Sybil's favor for selection by Wolf was that Dr. Patel was only an assistant professor of neurosurgery at Cornell University School of Medicine while Sybil was an associate professor, and she had a Ph.D..

The Wolf News Channel is located at 1000 Avenue of the Americas in New York, an easy commute for Sybil. Her professorship in Georgetown sparked an interest on the part of Wolf executives to establish a small satellite studio in D.C. to make it easier for them to capitalize on the federal government people who would then be more willing to appear on Wolf owing to the convenience. The RNC was going through a torturous restructuring to tone down the Tea Party influence and to make a shift that would bring them closer to the center. The Republican National Committee had only recently begun to see the handwriting on the wall that their extremist positions were going to destroy the party. Sybil's extensive relationships in the Latino community and with women's groups made her a perfect candidate for the Wolf News family which had a deserved reputation of being politically somewhere to the right of Genghis Khan, anti-progress, and anti-minorities. Sybil seemed to be the Goldilocks—not too left and not too right, but just right—choice for the plum job.

Sybil accepted both the George Washington University professorship and the Wolf News consultative position graciously, leaving the formal announcement to be part of the news as soon as she got settled in Georgetown, where she and Charles bought a large new home.

It was relatively easy for Sybil to transfer her active patient load to her partners, David Pennyman and Adele Sanchez-Hernandez. They had all taken turns when on-call to deal with each other's patients; so, both the neurosurgical partners and the patients were familiar with each other. Sybil was careful to send out the proper legal letters telling of her leaving the practice and recommending that they seek the services of other neurosurgeons, preferably to continue with her old partners. She saw her last patient in her clinic two weeks before actually departing from California.

The most difficult change in her life was saying goodbye to her partners in the horse breeding business.

She asked her friends and partners—Jose and Maria Innocenta Pomposo-Alvarez, Donita Pomposo Pancho and Carlita Rodriguez, and Marcos and Viviana Hernandez—to dinner. After the dessert dishes were cleared, she made her announcement and proposition.

"We have been friends and partners for a long time. You know I had a hard time with Bel Geddes and all of the suits and then the murder trial. What you don't know—and I trust you will keep my secret—is that the hospital kicked me out. I landed on my feet, but it would be very difficult for me to practice neurosurgery in California any longer. My husband has to relocate to New York, and I have been offered positions at Georgetown University and as a consultant on Wolf News. It is time for me to make a clean break. So, here is what I want to offer you guys. I sell you everything in the horse breeding ranch—land, buildings, equipment, stock, everything. Our lawyers and accountants can make a fair price. I don't have to have any serious money up front; so, maybe we could agree on a ten year buyout of my portion. What do you think?"

It came as a bolt from the blue; so, the Mexican-Americans had to have some time to think. The women compared their current status to the time when they first arrived on Sybil's property destitute and afraid, having just been cheated out of three month's wages by their employer. They all worried about taking on extra cost but; in the end, they thanked God, the Fortunes, and Sybil for the great opportunity they were getting. They agreed, and even arranged to buy the big house. In a couple of weeks, Sybil and her husband owned nothing in California.

Sybil was experienced and sophisticated. That made her self-confident, but she confided to her husband that she was scared. It was exciting to contemplate a new life in the East; but, by the same token, she was nervous about going off to personal uncharted country and an uncertain future.

-The End-

AUTHOR CARL DOUGLASS, a former neurosurgeon turned fulltime author, writes with gripping realism because in all his books he has been there and done that in some measure. He grew up in a small town where fighting was the rule, not the exception. He was determined to escape the sameness of geography, intellectual outlook, and career prospects of the majority of his contemporaries. In complete naiveté, he applied to only one well-known major university for his undergraduate work, and to everyone's surprise, he was accepted. He found himself out of his league scholastically and had to work like a Hannibal to find a way or make one to succeed in that rarefied atmosphere. His goal of success was to become a neurosurgeon, and he did it. His career in academia and the military as well as his work as a medical humanitarian provided the background to produce the riveting tales that have made their way into his remarkable books.

HONORS, AWARDS, AND MEMBERSHIPS
Phi Kappa Phi University Honor Society
Alpha Omega Alpha Medical Honor Society
BS (Medical Biology) degree—magna cum laude
MD—magna cum laude
CDR/MC/USN

American Medical Association
American Association of Neurosurgeons
Congress of Neurological Surgeons
Fellow of the American College of Surgeons
The Association of Military Surgeons of the United States
Life Member of the Medical Society of Vienna
Diplomate of the American Board of Neurological Surgery

Past President, Our Community Foundation, Wasatch
County, Utah
Past Medical Liaison Officer, Deseret International Foundation
Past Chief of Surgery,
Antelope Valley Regional Medical Center, Lancaster, California
Past Member-at-Large, Central Medical Committee,
Utah Valley Regional Medical Center, Provo, Utah
Past Member, Utah State Foster Care Review Committee

Sybil Norcroft Book Two

Uncharted Country, Uncertain Future

Wolf News receives an exclusive tip from a most unlikely source—a disgruntled WWN stringer, Jules Renier, who has ended up in the Congo. The most compelling aspect of Renier's report is that pygmy people of the area are being subjected to medical experimentations using highly infectious disease agents. Renier is adamant about secrecy. He does not want to see Raja Patel and the WWN news hordes descending into his village and taking all of the credit.

The Wolf studios are in a state of pandemonium trying to outdo their chief rival, WWN. Sybil Norcroft, M.D., Ph.D. could not have appeared on the scene at a more propitious time. Through no fault of her own, she lost her hospital and operating privileges in California and accepted a preliminary offer from Wolf to become the senior medical consultant for the network and to take on the immensely popular neurosurgeon/media star, Raza Patel, as his rival. Before her contract was even signed, the vice-president of the net-work tells her she is needed in the Congo and that she needs to leave the following day.